THE
STRANGER

<JOIN THE FIGHT>

ANIMORPHS™

ANIMORPHS™

THE STRANGER

K. A. APPLEGATE

SCHOLASTIC INC.

NEW YORK   TORONTO   LONDON   AUCKLAND
SYDNEY   MEXICO CITY   NEW DELHI   HONG KONG

For Michael

ISBN 978-0-545-42414-1

12 11 10 9 8 7 6 5 4 3 2 1   12 13 14 15 16 17/0

Printed in the U.S.A.   40

This edition first printing, June 2012

CHAPTER 1

My name is Rachel.

And you know the drill. I'm not going to tell you my last name. I'm not going to tell you where I live. I'll tell you all I can, because you need to know what's going on. You need to know what's happening.

But I need to stay alive. And if the Yeerks knew who I was, I would be dead.

Or worse.

The Yeerks are here. That's what you need to know.

People look up at the stars at night and wonder what it would be like if creatures from another planet ever landed on Earth.

1

Well, you can stop wondering. It's happened.

The Yeerks are parasites. They live in the brains of other species — humans, for example. They turn human beings into mindless slaves — Human-Controllers.

So when I say that the aliens are here, don't go looking around for some cute little thing like E.T. You won't see the Yeerks. They are parasitic worms, evil gray slugs that live in the heads of humans.

They can be in anyone. Your best friend. Your favorite teacher. The mayor of your town. Your brother. Sister. Mother. Father.

Anyone might be a Controller. You might be a Controller.

So I won't tell you my last name. Or where I live. But I will tell you the truth. The truth that only the Animorphs know.

Animorph. Animal morpher. A human capable of becoming any animal. It's our one weapon against the Yeerks. Our only power. Without it, we're just five regular kids.

But with that power comes certain extra responsibilities . . . as I was trying to explain to my best friend, Cassie.

It was a Sunday night. It was late. The circus had finished its last show. Their trailers and tents were clustered around the back side of the big City Arena.

The Arena is a place where they hold rock concerts and ice shows and play basketball games. And where they have circuses.

"Look, we both saw what we saw," I told Cassie. "Are you telling me it doesn't make you mad? That jerk using a cattle prod on an elephant doesn't make you mad?"

"Of course it does, Rachel," Cassie said. "I don't even like circuses."

"I don't, either. But my dad had tickets, and it was our big once-every-other-week, father-and-daughters thing. I had to come."

My dad had taken my sisters and me to see the circus earlier in the evening. See, my mom and dad are divorced, so my dad does these little outings where we all get together every second weekend. Sometimes it's just me and my dad. Like when we go hiking together, or go to ball games, or gymnastics events. Those are all things my dad and I like, but Jordan and Sara, my sisters, don't.

My little sisters loved the circus, but it's not my kind of thing. I guess I'm too old. That's why I dragged Cassie along. So I'd have someone to talk to when my sisters were getting all excited over the clowns and stuff.

Still, it was an opportunity to spend time with my

dad, which I enjoy. I don't get to see him as much as I wish I could. Everyone always says how much I'm like him. How he's kind of reckless, and so am I. He always seems so sure of himself, and I guess people think I'm that way, too. We're even both into gymnastics. My dad almost made the U.S. Olympic team when he was younger.

Of course, I've never told my father about my other life. I couldn't. But I wish I could. He would worry about me and all, but he would also think it was cool. My dad is very big on standing up for what's right. I think he would admire what I do. That would be nice, feeling like my dad admired me.

There wasn't much activity in the little tent-and-trailer city outside the Arena. I could hear dogs barking. I could hear raucous laughter coming from a brightly painted trailer. I could smell the usual circus smells — manure, hay, beer, cotton candy.

There were security guards around the perimeter of the area, but I wasn't worried about them. I've gone one-on-one with Hork-Bajir warriors. After you've fought one of those seven-foot-tall walking razor blades, regular old humans don't scare you much.

Cassie and I walked silently past the tiger cage. The three big cats just stared blankly. It was night. They wanted to be in the jungle. Instead they were in a too-small cage, trapped in a nightmare invented by humans.

Then I saw the elephant pen. There was a sturdy fence around four big Asian elephants. They were a little different from the African elephant I knew so well. But they were elephants, just the same.

I have sort of a special relationship with elephants.

Cassie and I had come to the elephant pen before the circus and seen the way their trainer treated them. He had used a cattle prod on them. It's a stick with a massive electrical shock. He used it to control the animals.

Later, during the show, he'd put on a big act of loving his elephants. But I'd seen the cattle prod. I just sat there, doing a slow boil all through the show. I knew I was going to have to take some action.

The elephant trainer's name was Josep something. Something hard to pronounce.

Well. He didn't know it yet, but Mr. Josep Something was about to have an eye-opening experience.

"See anyone around?" I asked Cassie.

"You know, Jake is going to read you the riot act over this," Cassie warned.

I laughed. "'Read the riot act?' That's like something my mother would say. What does it even mean?"

Cassie shrugged and smiled her shy smile. "I don't know. My dad says it all the time. I was trying to sound responsible and mature and parental."

"Look, I am *going* to do this," I said.

Cassie sighed. "Why did I let you talk me into *this*?"

"Because you know I'm right."

Cassie rolled her eyes. "Just don't hurt the guy, okay?"

"Me? Ms. Peace, Love, and Understanding? He'd just better not show up carrying that cattle prod, or I swear, I'll—"

I noticed Cassie had stopped walking. She was giving me her sorrowful look. Like she was ashamed of me.

I cringed. "Okay, okay. I'll just *talk* to the guy. Turn off the look. I hate that look. You're going to be a really good mother someday, with a look like that."

I found the gate in the elephant pen and opened it. I slipped inside while Cassie retreated into the shadows to watch my back. I moved slowly, not making any threatening moves that might alarm the elephants.

Elephants may be gentle, but they *are* big.

You don't want to be in the middle of four upset elephants.

I went to a far, dark corner of the pen and began the familiar ritual of focusing my mind. I concentrated on the elephant. *My* elephant. The elephant whose DNA was a part of me.

And then I began to change.

I felt the sprouting of my legs

CHAPTER 2

People say I'm pretty. I don't know and I really don't care. But I'll tell you one thing—no one who has ever seen me morph into an elephant ever used the word *pretty* to describe it.

I felt the thickening of my legs and arms.

I watched as my skin grew leathery and gray as mud.

I felt the sudden sprouting of my trunk as my nose and upper lip seemed to explode outward.

"Pinocchio, eat your heart out," Cassie whispered.

I felt the teeth in the front of my mouth run together, and then begin to grow and grow into long, spear-length tusks. It's a creepy sensation, by the way. Not painful, but definitely creepy.

I was growing big. More than big. I was gaining several thousand pounds.

Several *thousand* pounds.

I was about twelve or thirteen feet tall. I had ears like beach blankets. I had a little, ropy tail. I was a full-grown African elephant, and I was ready to have a little, um, talk with Mr. Josep Something.

"Hhhhuuuuhhhrrrooooooomm!"

I threw up my trunk and let go of a trumpet blast. It was the sound of a very angry elephant.

"You could have warned me," I heard Cassie whisper. "I almost wet myself over here."

It took about three minutes before the trainer came rushing into the pen. In the dark, all he saw were the gray shapes of his elephants. I wasn't exactly hiding, because, let's face it, when you're an elephant, you can't scrunch up and look small. But I was staying back until he was all the way inside the pen.

Then . . .

I lunged forward, pushing two of the other elephants aside.

The trainer gaped up at me. "What? What the . . . ?"

In a sudden, fluid movement, as he stared in puzzlement, I wrapped my trunk around his waist.

"Hey! Hey! You're not one of my elephants!"

Here's the thing about elephant trunks: They are so subtle that I can pick up an egg with my trunk and never crack it. Or I can pick up a tree and throw it across the yard.

Josep Something knew this.

I wrapped my trunk tightly around his waist and then I lifted him up off the ground. His feet kicked helplessly in the air. His arms pounded weakly on my trunk.

I lifted him up till he was at my eye level.

<Hi, Josep,> I said, using thought-speak.

"What the . . . ? Who? Who said that? I'm hearing voices!"

<Me,> I replied. <I said it. See, Josep, I am from the International Elephant Police. We have had some complaints about you.>

"This is crazy! This is *crazy*! What are you? Is this some sort of a joke?"

So I squeezed him a little tighter. Just enough so he couldn't really breathe very well.

<Now, listen to me. Because I could just as easily squeeze you out like a tube of toothpaste. So pay attention. You have been using cattle prods on your elephants. That is a no-no.>

10

"But . . ." he gasped. "They . . . are . . . my . . . property!"

This man was just not getting the message. So I extended my trunk a little and held him right over the tip of my left tusk. Like a worm about to be placed on a fishing hook.

<With one twitch of my trunk I can make you a shish kebab. *Now* are you going to listen to me?>

"Yes! Yes! I'm listening," he said. "I am listening very closely."

<No more cattle prods. No more pain of any kind. Do you understand me?>

"Y-y-y-yes."

<Because I'll be watching. And if you ever, *ever* hurt an elephant again . . . ever . . . I'll come back for you. And I will squeeze you till you pop like an over-cooked hot dog. Do you understand me?>

"Y-y-y-yes."

<Josep, can you fly?>

"What? Can I fly? No. No, of course not."

<I'll bet you can,> I said. And with that, I lowered my trunk almost to the ground. Then, with a sudden toss of my head and a deft twist of my trunk, I sent Josep Something flying.

He landed safely atop a tent. About, oh, twenty feet away.

"*Now* can we go home?" Cassie asked.

CHAPTER 3

"You threw the guy into the air?" Jake asked. "Wasn't that maybe just a little unnecessary?"

"No. He made me mad," I said.

It was the next day after school, a Monday. We were walking through the woods. Me, Cassie, Jake, Marco, and Tobias.

Of course, Tobias wasn't really walking. He was flying overhead in little hops from branch to branch. He stayed close so he could hear us. Red-tailed hawks have excellent hearing, but he still had to stay fairly close.

"Well, Rachel, you know I sympathize," Jake said

mildly, "but I don't think our job is really to right every wrong that's done to animals. That would be a full-time job, unfortunately."

I looked at Cassie. She gave me a wink. We kind of didn't tell Jake that she had been there, too. Cassie and Jake like each other. She didn't want him to be mad at her.

With me, it's a different story. Everyone knows I'm going to do whatever I feel like doing.

"We have other stuff to deal with," Marco grumbled. "The Andalite didn't give us this power so we could turn into the Animorph Society for the Prevention of Cruelty to Animals."

"Fine," I said. Which wasn't exactly like admitting I was wrong. "But what's got you so serious, Marco?"

"Let's wait till we find Ax. I don't want to have to tell the story twice."

So we tromped noisily on through the woods.

I felt a surge of excitement. You couldn't miss the tension in Marco's voice. Something was up. There was the smell of danger in the air, and that meant action.

I like action. I like *doing* things instead of just talking about them. Marco makes fun of me over it. He calls me Xena, Warrior Princess.

But I'm not one of those morons who is just into danger for its own sake. It's not about cheap thrills.

It's about feeling like I am involved in something very important. I mean, let's face it—as corny as it sounds, we are trying to help save the world.

It began months ago. The five of us just happened to get together at the mall. It's not like we were a group, really. Not before that night.

Jake's my cousin, but we never hung out together much. Jake's sort of in charge. It's not something he ever asked for; it's just that he's good at dealing with responsibility. He's the kind of person you automatically turn to if there's a crisis. And probably the best thing about him is that he can tell people what to do without ever sounding bossy.

"Since when don't you want to tell the same story twice?" Jake teased Marco. "I've known you to tell the same tired jokes eighty or ninety times."

"It's your own fault," Marco said. "If you would just laugh the first time, I wouldn't have to keep telling them."

Marco is Jake's best friend. He's smaller than Jake, funnier, darker, more skeptical. But his suspicious nature makes him very good at seeing beneath the surface of things. And as much as he whines and complains about the dangerous situations we get into, he's still there in the worst of the fight, still making dumb jokes.

Marco has changed lately, at least a little. He

doesn't resist being an Animorph like he used to. I don't know why. Maybe it's because his dad finally seems to have gotten over the death of Marco's mother. I don't know.

"Hey, look! Over by that tree. See? A baby skunk with its mother." Cassie, of course. No one else would notice, or get excited over, skunks.

"Let's run right over and pet them," Marco said.

Cassie laughed. "I've handled skunks plenty of times and never been sprayed."

"Yeah, well, that's you, Dr. Dolittle."

Cassie has been my best friend forever. I have no idea why. No one does, because we seem like we would never get along. Cassie lives on a farm. Both her parents are veterinarians. She spends all her free time in the Wildlife Rehabilitation Clinic her dad runs in their barn. They save injured animals.

Cassie is very into animals, but she's not one of those animal lovers who can't stand people. She just thinks of humans as a different species of animal.

Then there is Tobias. Back when all this started, Tobias was barely an acquaintance of Jake and Marco, although I kind of knew him. He was a sweet, poetic kind of guy. The kind bullies love to pick on. He used to have messy, out-of-control hair and dreamy eyes that always seemed to be looking at something no one else could see.

15

Used to . . .

Now he has fierce, angry eyes that look through you like laser beams. Now he has brownish feathers, and a white chest, and a reddish tail, and cruel-looking talons, and a wickedly curved beak.

Tobias was trapped in a morph. Now, he's a red-tailed hawk. A predator who lives on mice and rabbits and sometimes other birds.

I still see him as sweet, gentle Tobias. But he has been a hawk for a long time now.

The gift of the Andalite, the power to morph, is a wonderful weapon. But like any weapon, it can destroy those who use it.

<Here he comes,> Tobias called down in the thought-speak we use when we are in a morph. <I think he sees us.>

I heard the sound of fallen leaves being stirred, a faint drumbeat of pounding hooves on pine needles.

Then, with a leap, he cleared a fallen tree trunk and landed a few feet away from us.

Aximili-Esgarrouth-Isthill. We call him "Ax" for short. The sole survivor of the destroyed Andalite Dome ship. The only living Andalite on planet Earth.

Ax is the brother of Prince Elfangor, the Andalite who warned us about the Yeerk invasion and gave us the power to morph. Prince Elfangor, who was destroyed by Visser Three, leader of the Yeerk forces on Earth.

<Hello, Prince Jake,> Ax said. <Hello, all.>

As much as I know Ax, and even consider him a friend, it's always a little bit of a shock to see him.

He looks like some odd cross of a human, a deer, and a scorpion. But not really like any of those things.

His upper body and head are more or less the human-looking parts. He has thin arms and many-fingered hands. His face is flat, with slits for a nose and two large almond eyes. He has no mouth at all, which is why thought-speak is the natural language of Andalites.

From atop his head rise two stalks, each with an eye on the end. He can turn these eyes in any direction he wants. They're completely independent of his main eyes.

His body is that of a pale blue and tan deer, or a thin pony. He has four legs that end in hooves. But his back slopes down, so that you would never be tempted to think of riding him.

And he has a tail. A long, thick, powerful tail that ends in a deadly scythe-shaped blade. I've seen him use that tail. He can strike so fast that the human eye sees nothing but a blur.

"Hey, Ax," Marco said. "How's it going?"

<It is going wonderfully. I was up in the hills

yesterday, and I was attacked by one of those very large cats. What do you call them? Cougars? It was very exciting.>

"Are you okay?" I asked.

<Certainly, Rachel. And I did not hurt the cougar, Cassie. Not fatally, anyway. But he won't try to eat me again, I think.> Ax gave his strange Andalite smile, an expression he managed even without a mouth.

Marco rolled his eyes. "I'm telling you, Ax and Rachel belong together. The two of you are sick. Someday you could get married while bungee-jumping into an active volcano."

I squirmed a little. Not because I minded Marco thinking I was bold. But because I really was not interested in Ax that way.

"Okay, now that we're all here, Marco, maybe you could tell us *why* we're all here," Jake said.

"I have some news," Marco began. "Actually, Tobias and I have some news."

I glanced up at Tobias, sitting in the tree. Of course he showed no expression. He just fixed his piercing gaze on Marco.

Marco swaggered just a bit as we formed a circle around him.

"It's a tale of initiative and courage and, yes, brilliance," Marco began.

"No, no, no. Just tell us, Marco," I snapped. "Don't try to milk the suspense."

"Okay," he said with an easy laugh. "My fellow Animorphs . . . and visiting alien . . . we have found a way into the Yeerk pool."

CHAPTER 4

"An entrance to the Yeerk pool?" I echoed. "Where? How?"

I looked around at the others to see their reactions. See, we had already invaded the Yeerk pool in an effort to save Jake's brother, Tom. Not a happy memory.

I saw Cassie shudder.

"Ax is the only one who wasn't there for our little vacation in the Yeerk pool," Marco said. "As the rest of you know, the Yeerk pool is in a huge underground cavern. It's practically a small city down there. It's under our school, but it's so big that it also runs beneath the fire station, a couple of gas stations, and most of the mall."

Ax nodded. <Yeerk pools are generally very large and elaborate. They are an important part of Yeerk life. The centers of their lives, really, almost like a religion. The pools are, for the Yeerks, what forests and meadows are to Andalites.>

"Tobias and I have been working out a pattern of surveillance," Marco went on. "For the last week, we've followed our very favorite Human-Controller, Assistant Principal Chapman, everywhere we can. Tobias tracks him from the air. Then I follow him when he goes into a building."

"Why didn't you let the rest of us in on this?" I demanded.

Marco shrugged. "It was a two-person job, that's all."

Jake looked as annoyed as I felt.

Then I realized why Marco had kept this quiet. Jake had just been through the terrifying ordeal of being infested by a Yeerk. For three days he had been a Human-Controller, a prisoner in his own body. Marco had been letting him rest.

"So?" I asked, a little more patiently.

"So what?" Marco answered.

"So where is this entrance to the Yeerk pool? Duh."

"Well, I was hoping to amaze and entertain you all with the whole story of our brilliant detective work, but the short answer is — in a dressing room at The Gap. In the mall. That's the entrance. People go in, looking like they're going to try on clothes, and they never come out."

<At least they don't come out *through* The Gap,> Tobias added. <They come out through the movie theater. When the crowd leaves the movie at the end of the show, there are always more people leaving than went in.>

"In through The Gap, out through the multiplex." Marco laughed. "Are these Yeerks on top of popular American culture, or what?"

"Good job," Jake admitted grudgingly. "The question is, now what do we do?"

<Attack!> Ax said instantly.

"We tried that once," Cassie said quietly. "We didn't exactly win. There were dozens of Hork-Bajir and Taxxons down there. And Human-Controllers. And *he* was there . . . Visser Three. That's when Tobias was trapped in a morph. Like I said, we didn't exactly win."

"We got hammered," I agreed. "Ax, you know I'm usually all for going on the attack, but the Yeerk pool is just too big."

<A warrior is judged by the power of his

22

enemies,> Ax said stubbornly. But he didn't sound quite as enthusiastic anymore.

"Attacking the Yeerk pool is out," I muttered. But an idea was occurring to me. "Hey, Ax? What can you tell us about the Kandrona?"

He swiveled his head toward me, while his stalk eyes turned slowly this way and that, searching the woods for trouble. <The Kandrona is a miniature version of the Yeerks' home sun. It emits Kandrona rays, which concentrate in the Yeerk pools. It is what nourishes the Yeerks. That is why the Yeerks must swim in their natural state in the Yeerk pool every three days — they need Kandrona rays.>

"So their real weakness is not the pool itself, but this Kandrona," I said. "This miniature sun."

<But the Kandrona may be many miles away from the Yeerk pool itself,> Ax explained. <The Kandrona rays may be beamed to the pool from almost any-where. So, although I am in favor of attacking the Yeerk pool, we should not do it expecting to find the Kandrona there.>

"I agree," I said. "But what if we didn't *attack* the Yeerk pool? What if we just spied it out? We might find out where the Kandrona is."

Marco laughed. "That's more like the Rachel I know. You were starting to worry me there. You were sounding so sensible."

"How big is a Kandrona?" Jake wondered.

<It would depend on how many pools it had to support. It might be as large as Cassie's barn. It might be the size of one of your human cars.>

"The size of a car? Surely a bunch of all-American kids like us could manage to wreck a car," Marco joked.

"How much would it hurt the Yeerks?" I asked. "That's the question. Is it worth running the risk of going down there again? Down to the Yeerk pool?"

We all looked at Ax.

<It would depend. If they have a spare Kandrona, it wouldn't hurt them very much. In any case, they have one aboard their mother ship, so we would not wipe them out entirely.>

We all sagged with disappointment.

<However, it would not be practical for the Yeerks to shuttle their Human-Controllers back and forth to the mother ship to keep them alive.>

"So what would they do?" Marco wondered. "How would Visser Three react?"

"Visser Three is totally ruthless," I said. "He would save as many as he could. But he'd have to let the rest die."

<Yes,> Ax agreed. <It would be a very serious blow. They would survive, but they would be weakened.>

"We'd have to find this Kandrona thing first," Cassie reminded everyone. "And wherever it is, it will be guarded."

Right then I guess we all realized we were going to do it. We were going back to the Yeerk pool.

Jake shook his head slowly. "Down to the Yeerk pool again. I still have nightmares about the first time."

"Yeah," Marco agreed. "Done that."

"The Yeerk pool," Cassie said grimly, and looked away.

I didn't say anything. I don't like talking about nightmares. But I'd had them, too. They were pretty bad.

<I am not very good at understanding human emotions,> Ax said. <But you all seem afraid. And *your* fear is beginning to scare *me*.>

"Good," I said. "I don't know if you Andalites believe in places like heaven and hell. But let me just tell you — the Yeerk pool is definitely not heaven."

CHAPTER 5

"What's for dinner?" I asked my mom as soon as I got home. The walk in the woods had made me hungry. Being outdoors always does that to me.

So does fear. I just kept picturing the Yeerk pool. The cages full of involuntary hosts, humans and Hork-Bajir, temporarily free of their Yeerk parasites.

I kept hearing them. Crying—that's what most of them did while they waited to be reinfested. Others screamed. Some begged for mercy.

Or worse.

My mom was standing by the kitchen counter. She was more dressed up than she usually was in the evening. She was munching nervously on some Doritos and kind of staring off into space.

"Mom? Hello?"

She looked like she hadn't noticed me. "Oh, hi, honey."

"What's for dinner? I'm starving."

"Your father is coming over tonight. For dinner. He said he would pick something up."

I felt my stomach clench. Something was wrong.

Since the divorce, my dad never came over for dinner. My two sisters and I spent one weekend a month overnight at his apartment in the city. Plus the every-other-weekend outing.

But he did not come over for dinner.

I wasn't hungry anymore. "What's going on?" I demanded.

My mother got this worried look on her face, which she tried to hide. "Your father has something he wants to tell you girls. He was supposed to tell you the other night at the circus. I guess he forgot."

The way she said "I guess he forgot" made it clear she didn't think that was the truth.

I took my mother's arm. "Mom? I don't like suspense, all right? So just—"

The doorbell rang.

I heard Sara running down the stairs. I heard Jordan yell, "Stop running on the stairs, you'll break

27

your neck." She sounded just like my mother. It almost made my mom and me smile.

"That will be your father."

I went to the front room. Sara was leaping into my dad's arms and Jordan was hovering a couple feet away. Jordan shot a quick, questioning glance at me. Unlike Sara, Jordan was old enough to realize something was up.

I shrugged and shook my head.

"Rachel!" my dad said. "How's my girl? Come take this bag from me. Thai food. We have curry. We have pad Thai. We have chicken satay. We have those imperial heavenly whatever-they-call-'em shrimp."

He handed me the paper bag. He was being too cheerful.

My father's a reporter for one of the local TV channels. He does a lot of investigative journalism. Plus he anchors the news on Saturday and Sunday. So he's always wearing nice clothes, and always has great hair, and he looks tan even in the total depths of winter.

I took the bag to the dining-room table and started to unpack the little white boxes of Thai food.

"Hello, Dan," my mother said, coming into the room with plates and silverware.

"Naomi," he answered. "How have you been?"

By now even Sara had figured out that this was not going to be a happy evening.

We ate a little and struggled along with some small talk about nothing. Until finally my mom said, "Dan, just get it over with."

My dad looked embarrassed. He sent me a sheepish smile, like some little boy caught doing something wrong.

"Okay," he said. He cleared his throat. He sat up straight in his chair. Just as if he were waiting for the cameras to come on so he could do the evening news.

"Kids, I have something I have to tell you about. I've been offered a job. A better job. I wouldn't just be the weekend anchor. I would have the top spot. I'd be anchoring the six o'clock broadcast *and* the eleven o'clock. And I'd get to do specials. Maybe do some really important work."

Jordan looked at me, confused. It *sounded* like good news.

"There's just one problem," my father said. "It's not here in town. In fact, it would mean I would have to move."

"Where to?" Sara asked. "To another apartment?"

He forced a smile. "To another city, sweetie. In another state."

"A thousand miles away," my mother said.

You know, it's funny how the mind works. See, I've been through more bad things, more terror, more worry, more pain since I became an Animorph than most people deal with in a lifetime. I would have thought I could handle something like my dad moving away.

A thousand miles away.

"Congratulations," I said, trying not to show any emotion. "It's what you've always wanted."

My dad wasn't fooled. He knew I was upset. "It's the job, Rachel. It's the way it is. It's not like I won't see you kids. I know it sounds like a long way and all, but that's why we have jets, right?"

"Yeah," I said. "That's why we have jets. I think I'll just go upstairs and do some homework now."

"Wait, I need to . . ." my dad protested.

I didn't slam any doors. I didn't throw anything. I just left.

Let *him* feel what it's like, I told myself. Let *him* feel what it's like to have someone just walk away.

I went up to my room and locked the door behind me. I couldn't breathe. I kept clenching my fists and wanting to pound something. I think I would have cried, but I was just too angry.

"Rachel?" It was him. He knocked lightly on my door. "Can I come in?"

I couldn't say no. It would have sounded like I was upset. "Sure. Why not?"

I unlocked the door, and he came in. "I'm guessing you're a little upset," he said.

I shrugged and turned my back to him.

"I see. Rachel, you didn't let me finish what I had to tell you downstairs. Rachel . . . Jordan and Sara are still too young to consider this. But you're older. You can look after yourself when I have to work late. They can't. And . . . anyway, look, the thing is, I've talked to your mother about this, and she's not happy about it, but she says it's up to you."

I turned to look at him. "*What's* up to me?"

He smiled uncertainly. "Well, it's like this. Carla Belnikoff teaches in the city I'm moving to. You know, she takes in three or four promising gymnastics students every year. If you wanted . . . well, it would be the best thing in the world, as far as I'm concerned, if you came to live with me."

I almost asked him to repeat it. I couldn't believe I had heard right the first time. Students of Coach Belnikoff have won two gold medals and a bunch of silver ones.

"Dad, Carla Belnikoff isn't going to take me on as a student. She handles professional-level gymnasts. I'm too tall, and not good enough to . . . besides, you're saying I should move out? Leave Mom and Sara and Jordan?"

"You're the only one who can decide that," my

31

dad said. "But as for Coach Belnikoff, you're wrong. You have the talent. I know. If that's something you want to do, if you want to make that your life, you could go places in gymnastics."

I shook my head. Not to say no, just to try and clear out the confusion. "Dad, are you asking me to go with you when you move?"

"Yes. I know it would be hard on you and your mom and your sisters, but we could make it work. I mean, this job pays a lot of money. You could fly back here any time you wanted. Every week if you wanted."

Was he serious? It sounded ridiculous. Was he actually serious? I sat down on the edge of my bed. My thoughts were everywhere all at once. Leave? Leave my mom and my sisters?

This was just because my dad felt guilty. He felt bad about leaving. This was about pity. He felt sorry for me or something.

"And I know it would mean changing schools," he said, "but, gee, Rachel, I think it could be okay, you know? I mean, for one thing, they have serious mountains there. We could do some rock climbing together on weekends. Go hiking. And it's a huge sports town. I need someone to go with me to games. It would be like in the old days." Then he winked. "And, hey, it's a much bigger city, so think of all the shopping."

No, it wasn't pity or guilt, I realized. At least not completely. I think my dad was feeling lonely. He was picturing himself lonely in the new town.

"Oh, man," I said. "I don't know what to say."

My dad nodded his head. "Don't decide now. I wouldn't want you to. Talk to your mom. And Jordan and Sara, too. You think about it. I think . . . you know, I've just missed you, sweetheart. We have fun trash-talking the umpires at games, don't we? And hiking? Remember the time we got lost?"

"Of course, I remember," I said. "I just . . . I have to think it over. You know."

I wanted to say, Dad, you don't understand. It isn't just about Mom and Sara and Jordan. I have a date, Dad. To go back to the Yeerk pool. My friends are counting on me. See, I'm supposed to be Xena, Warrior Princess. I'm supposed to go back down there . . . down into the last place on Earth I want to go.

"I have to think it over," I repeated.

"Yeah. So. Anyway, I'm gonna go now."

"Okay, Dad," I said.

"I love you, Rachel."

I wish he hadn't said that. I was doing fine till he said that, and then the tears started.

CHAPTER 6

After my dad left, I talked to my mom. She said what I expected: She wanted me to stay. But it was up to me. She trusted me to think it through.

Up to me. Great. I could hurt my mom and my sisters, or I could hurt my dad. Perfect. Isn't divorce fun?

After I went to bed, I just lay there, staring up at the ceiling. My brain kept churning like a computer you can't turn off. Too many things to think about. My dad. My mom.

And the big, huge, massive thing I didn't even want to start thinking about: my friends. The Animorphs. The war against the Yeerks.

Finally, I knew I had to get out of there. I needed air and open spaces. The walls were just way too close around me.

I climbed out of bed and opened my window all the way. I changed from the T-shirt I sleep in to the black leotard I usually wore under my clothes.

My morphing outfit.

I couldn't think about it anymore. I just needed some space to not think about my father. Not think about choices.

I focused my mind. I concentrated. Just some time to think, I told myself, as my fingers became feathers and my toes curled into talons.

I guess every kid has times he wants to just get away. But I had the power to do it. I could even get away from myself.

I launched myself into the night. I flew in absolute silence. The wind rushing over the top of my wings never ruffled a feather.

The moon was low on the horizon, just a sliver. High clouds blocked the starlight. The grassy field just a few feet below me would have been black and featureless to human eyes.

But I was not looking through human eyes.

My eyes were so large, they nearly filled my head. They looked through the darkness like it was noon on a sunny day. I could see individual blades of grass.

I could see the ants crawling beneath the grass.

My hearing was so acute that I could hear a mouse step on a twig from seventy-five feet away. I could hear the beating wings of a sparrow that was flitting from tree to tree.

I had morphed into a great horned owl. The night killer. The predator of darkness.

I flew lower still, closer to the ground, letting the owl's mind search out prey. Here a mouse. There a shrew. There a vole. And all the many little birds.

They were all meat to the owl. I could descend, silent and deadly, on a rat or rabbit, spread my talons wide, and strike.

I could squeeze my talons until they burst the skulls of my prey and . . . no. No, I told myself. I was not Tobias. He had no choice but to be a predator. I had a choice.

Like my father had a choice. He could just not move. And then I wouldn't have to make this awful decision. If he knew . . . if he understood everything . . . he wouldn't do this. He would understand that I was part of the battle to help save Earth.

But I couldn't tell him. Not even my dad. He could be one of them. That's what knowing about the Yeerks does to you. You look at everyone and wonder what's living inside their brains. Even though I felt like somehow I would just know if my dad were a Controller.

I guess I've always had a close relationship with my dad. Right from the start, going back as far as I can remember, we were always doing stuff together. I mean, I have this photograph of me when I was three years old, standing on a balance beam, with my dad holding me up and grinning at the camera. I love that picture, even though I look lame in the outfit I had on. I keep it on my desk in my room.

When my mom was pregnant with my littlest sister, Sara, I overheard my parents talking. My mom was saying maybe this time she would have a boy. "I know you've always wanted a boy," she told my dad.

"Oh, come on," he answered. "That was years ago. I thought I had to have a boy to do all the fun 'dad' stuff with. But I have Rachel. She's as good as any boy. She's already tougher than most boys her age. Have you seen the vaults she can do?"

My mom groaned. "Don't *ever* let her hear you say that. Little girls do *not* want to be told they are as good as a boy."

But she was wrong. I know it was sexist and all, but I still just thought it was great. My dad thought I was as tough as any boy. Cool.

If only he knew what I was doing now, I thought.

How could he expect me to make this decision? I couldn't leave my friends. I couldn't. They were counting on me. We were going back to the Yeerk pool, and they were counting on me to be brave and strong. That's what they thought I was.

But if I was so brave and so strong, why was I suddenly imagining a very different life, a long, long way from the war with the Yeerks?

Why was I imagining a life of gymnastics classes and ball games with my dad — a place where I was just a person? Where no one expected me to go back down into that hell of screams and despair called the Yeerk pool?

If I was so brave and so tough, why was I imagining a normal life?

CHAPTER 7

I flew into Tobias's territory. It was also the territory of at least one real horned owl, who would not be happy to have me around. It belonged to Tobias by day and to the owl by night.

I knew a tree where Tobias often slept. Sure enough, he was there. I stopped beating my wings and glided up.

I was already flaring my wings to come in for a landing when Tobias noticed me.

<It's okay, it's okay, it's me, Rachel!>

<Oh, man! You almost gave me a heart attack!>

<Sorry.>

<Sorry?!> he demanded angrily. <It's night, we're in the woods, I'm a hawk and you're an owl who comes zooming up in attack mode. Don't do that kind of stuff, Rachel.>

<I'm just an owl, not an eagle,> I protested. I knew that some eagles and some falcons will attack hawks.

<Okay, okay. It's just that hungry owls have been known to go after hawks. It doesn't happen a lot, but owls scare me. I know everybody sees cute cartoon owls and thinks all they do is say 'hoot, hoot' and act wise. But let me tell you, I've watched owls work. They aren't cute. They're tough. I don't ever want to have to fight one.>

I settled on the branch beside him, sinking my talons into the soft bark. I could see why Tobias liked this perch. It gave a perfect view of the meadow, with all its tasty prey.

<I'm really sorry, Tobias. I guess I forget that your life can be so dangerous.>

<Yeah, well, it has advantages, too,> he said. <No more first-period gym class. So what are you doing out here playing owl?>

<I had to get out of the house.>

<Ah. Why? Unless it's not any of my business.>

<I don't know. Nothing. Nothing. I was just

hyper.> Tobias didn't say anything. Obviously, he knew I was lying. He just waited for me to tell him, watching me with gold-brown eyes that seemed to drill holes through me.

But I didn't really want to tell him. I mean, I guess I *had* wanted to, or why else would I have flown out to see him? But now it just seemed ridiculous to lay my problems on him.

<I was just thinking about going down into the Yeerk pool again,> I said.

<You're worried?> he teased. <You?>

<I get worried sometimes,> I said defensively. <I was thinking about flying out to The Gardens, to the zoo. Maybe acquiring some new morph. Something really strong and mean in case we get into a fight down there. A lion. Or a grizzly bear or something. Thought maybe you'd want to fly over there with me.>

<Rachel, you know I don't fly much at night. I can't see that well in the dark. Plus there aren't any thermals at night, so I can't soar. I just have to flap the whole time, and that's miles away. I mean, a little trip around here, sure, if you want to go flying. But that's a haul.>

<Yeah, okay. Forget it.>

<I have an idea. Why don't you tell me what's

really bothering you? You're all . . . weird. You don't seem like you.>

<It's nothing,> I said. <Sorry I scared you. I'm going to head on home.>

<Rachel, you know you can always talk to me, right?>

<Yeah. Look . . . I have a question for you. Do you ever think about years from now? Like when it's time for college and stuff?> As soon as the words were out of my head I wished I could call them back.

But Tobias was cool. He just laughed silently. <Yeah, I'm thinking I could get easy As in — ornithology — the study of birds.>

<You could definitely be the professor,> I said. <I just meant that sooner or later most of us are going to leave. Move somewhere else. What do we do then, if the Yeerks are still around?>

Tobias began preening his feathers. It's something he has to do, but it's also a habit he has when he's bothered by something. <I haven't really looked that far ahead. But I guess I figured this whole thing would sort itself out, one way or the other, long before then. The Yeerks win, and you don't have to worry about college. Or they lose, and we each go back to our normal lives. Some of us more normal than others,> he added dryly.

For a while I didn't say anything. I couldn't.

42

I was too busy hating myself for bringing this up with Tobias. Tobias, of all people! He was already a casualty in this war. He was trapped in a hawk morph. And here I was thinking of bailing out?

What was the matter with me? I couldn't leave. Leave Tobias living in the forest? Leave my best friend, Cassie, to fight, maybe to die, so I could cut and run? Leave Jake and Marco and Ax? Why? Because my dad was lonely and I could take gymnastics classes?

<Rachel? You okay?>

No. I wasn't okay. I felt sick. What was the matter with me? I couldn't leave. I couldn't give up. <Me? Of course I'm okay,> I lied. <Just the same, I think I will go get myself some firepower. It's time for *Yeerk Pool Two: Animorphs' Revenge*, right?>

<I don't know. It looks like I'll be sitting out this battle,> Tobias said.

<Don't worry,> I said. <I'll get a Hork-Bajir for you.>

<You're okay? Really? It seemed like you were upset.>

<Tobias, I am more than okay. Gotta go.>

<Rachel, go *home*,> Tobias advised.

I opened my wings and beat them powerfully, sliding through the dead air of night.

But I did not go home. I flew around a while, trying to get a grip on the confusion in my head. But I
couldn't. And I couldn't go home yet. I knew I would
just lie there in bed, eyes wide open.

I turned and headed south.

CHAPTER 8

From the air, The Gardens looks very different than it does from the ground. The roller coaster doesn't look nearly as tall or scary. And flying above the zoo area, you mostly just see the roofs of the various interior exhibits. The rest of it seems, at first, to be sparse woods, with cement pathways winding in and around and through, like curled ribbons.

Looking closer, I could see the separate habitats. The trees and the running stream of the tiger area. The open field for the bison, separated by a tall fence from the impalas.

I glided over to the lions. Most were sleeping by

a tree. One female was ranging around restlessly, like she was looking for something.

It took a while to find the bears. I wasn't interested in the little black bears. Or the polar bears. I was looking for the grizzlies.

I wanted power.

There they were in a habitat of trees and rocks and a deep water-filled moat fed by a tumbling, rushing stream.

There were two, a male and female pair. Both were asleep, sprawled across the rocks. The male was bigger. That's what I wanted. Big. Powerful. Fearless. If I was going back to the Yeerk pool, I wanted something desperately dangerous.

Leave? Move out of town? Give up? No way.

No way.

And my dad? I would still see him when he came to town. That's what jets were for.

I landed and began to morph back. To revert to my true human form. My feathers melted and ran together and became pink. My beak broke into teeth. My talons became smooth toes. My insides gurgled and squished and sloshed as some organs grew and others changed and others reappeared from nothing.

The bear heard the sounds of my bones stretching, and the faint rustle of feathers melting together to become flesh. He opened one eye and looked at me without understanding or fear.

He was well fed. He had been in the zoo for many years, and had all but forgotten the wariness of living in the wild. I was just something that smelled a little like a bird and a little like a human.

I reached a trembling human hand down to touch the rough coat of the grizzly bear. His nearsighted eyes watched me. I was nothing to him. I could not hurt him. He could destroy me without bothering even to wake up fully.

He was beyond fear. Beyond doubt. Beyond pain.

"It must be nice," I whispered to him.

I touched him and felt his power flow into me.

And yet, as I absorbed his DNA and imagined myself becoming this fearless creature, I still could not forget the look in my father's eyes, or the quaver in his voice saying, "But, gee, Rachel, I think it could be okay, you know?"

I could already feel the emptiness his moving would leave in my life. He could say he'd come back every other week. He could say we'd still see each other just as much. But I knew it wouldn't be that way.

I could imagine him packing up to go.

I could remember the screams in the Yeerk pool.

I could remember Tobias trying to joke about college.

Too much. Things that were small and personal, and things that were huge, all swirled together in my head. Nothing made sense. It was too much stuff. Too much fear and guilt and loneliness. Too many decisions. Too much.

You know, there are days when I just don't feel brave and fearless. There are days when I just want to go to a ball game with my dad and eat popcorn and tune out everything else that's going on. Be a normal kid.

But that wasn't the life I had. Not anymore.

CHAPTER 9

The next evening, as planned, we all arrived at the mall separately. I met up with Cassie at the food court.

"Hi. What a huge surprise to see you here," I said.

"Uh-huh."

We did a little act for any curious Controller who might be watching, pretending to be surprised to see each other. I looked at my watch. "Perfect. We have fifteen minutes to wander slowly toward The Gap."

"I saw Jake and Ax down playing video games," Cassie said. "Poor Jake. You know how unpredictable Ax is when he's in human morph. While I was watching, he tried to eat a stray cigarette butt off the floor."

Andalites have no mouths and no sense of taste. So whenever Ax played human, he found the sense of taste extremely exciting. He would try to eat everything around him.

I laughed at the image of Ax chewing on a cigarette butt. I was surprised I *could* laugh. This was not a mission I was looking forward to.

We arrived at the store.

"Marco says it's in the last dressing room," I reminded Cassie. "And we have to assume the people who work here in the store are all Controllers. Speaking of Marco, I wonder if he made it on time?"

"I'm sure he did," Cassie said. "He seems to be kind of into all this lately."

"Yeah, what's that about?" I muttered.

Cassie shrugged. "People change, I guess. I feel sorry for Tobias, not being able to come along. It'll tear him up. On the other hand, I'm jealous."

I nodded in agreement. I was feeling hyper again. Jazzed. The way I usually did before we set out to do something dangerous. Only more so this time. I'll admit it—the Yeerk pool scared me. The idea of that awful place made me sick at heart. And now we were going back down there.

"Time to go to the dressing room," I said. "Pick something out you want to try on."

Cassie looked at me blankly. "Like what?"

I rolled my eyes. Cassie cannot shop. She is shopping-impaired. "Just pretend you're me. Grab a sweater or something."

I spotted Jake and Ax across the room. Ax's human morph is always a little surprising to see because it's a combination of DNA from Jake, Marco, Cassie, and me. He's a guy, but sort of pretty, and with a definite hint of weirdness about him.

I grabbed a sweater for Cassie and held it out for her.

"Like I would ever wear *that*," she said. "It says 'dry clean only.'"

We went to the next-to-last dressing room and closed the door behind us.

"Let's do this," I said tersely.

We had all decided the best way to go was in cockroach morph. The last time we'd morphed into roaches, things had not gone well. But roaches were fast, and their senses were good enough to use for our purposes. Also, they might go unnoticed.

I was not looking forward to doing the roach body again. I don't like becoming anything that can be stepped on. Besides, if you think *looking* at a cockroach is gross, try *being* one.

I looked at Cassie and let out a yelp. Two hugely long antennae were sprouting from her forehead.

"Jeez, you could have warned me you were starting."

Morphing is not some neat, sensible process where you just gradually become something else. It is much weirder than that. Different changes happen at different times. Body parts appear suddenly, other parts disappear. And the sizes don't always match up till the end.

The first change on Cassie was the sudden appearance of the antennae, which shot straight out of her forehead like two fishing poles.

Then her skin started to get crispy-looking.

At the same time, we were both shrinking, which feels just like falling. I mean, you see the walls shooting up, higher and higher. You see the ground rushing up at you like you're a parachutist whose chute didn't open.

Unfortunately, since it was a dressing room, there were mirrors on two sides.

"AAHHH!" I cried, startled by the nauseating sight of the skin of my back melting into two huge, hard, brown wings.

Cassie was too far gone to say "shh," but she held one of her hands up to what was left of her lips. Just then her extra legs came popping out of her stomach, and I think I would have yelped again except that I no longer had a mouth.

I heard a slurping sound as the last of my bones dissolved, and I sagged into my exoskeleton.

My clothing was piled around me like a huge collapsed tent.

Human sight was gone now. What I could see was vague and muddy and shattered into a thousand pieces. But I'd had practice being a roach. I could make some sense of the roach's confusing way of seeing.

And there were compensations. The antennae that had sprouted from my head were amazingly good at reading vibrations and smells.

<You okay?> I asked Cassie.

<I'm trapped under my own jeans,> she said. <No, wait. There. I'm out.>

<I see you,> I said. <Yikes! Look out! There are pins all over the carpet.>

The straight pins were steel shafts that looked as big around as the crossbar of a swing set. The sharp ends didn't seem very sharp at this size. And the blunt ends were like big steel beach balls.

<Okay, let's get out of the way,> I said.

We scurried on our six legs over to a corner underneath the small triangular seat.

<Man, this roach brain really wants to run,> Cassie said.

<Tell me about it,> I agreed. When you first

morph an animal, it is almost always a struggle to adjust to its particular instincts. We had morphed roaches before, so we were prepared, but the first time I had become a roach it was all I could do to control the panic.

Even now, the roach's jumpy instincts were barely under control. "Run!" it said. "Run!"

I heard loud, crashing vibrations. Something huge moved over our heads. I couldn't see well enough to recognize him, but a few seconds later he began to morph down into our world.

<Who is that?> I asked.

<Me, Marco. What, you don't recognize me?>

After that came Ax, who had to morph back into his Andalite body and then into a roach. Jake grabbed all the clothing we had shed, stuffed it into a bag, and took it away to store in one of the coin lockers out in the mall. Then he came back and morphed into his own cockroach form. His own outer clothing would be sacrificed, left in the dressing room. That would look strange, but not as strange as five separate sets of clothing.

<Okay, boys, girls, and bugs,> Marco said, <this has taken about fifteen minutes, which means we are already down to an hour and forty-five minutes in morph. And this is NOT a morph I want to be stuck in.>

<Amen. Let's move out,> Jake said.

We scampered like a very tiny, very gross army beneath the divider that separated us from the next dressing room. This was the dressing room Marco believed led to the Yeerk pool.

<We can hide up under the seat,> I said.

One of the cooler parts of being a roach is the ability to walk right up most walls. We shot up the wall and cowered beneath the roof formed by the little triangular seat.

I rested, facing straight up on the wall. Tiny spines at the end of my legs gripped the small bumps of the painted wall. I could see two of the others just above me, parked like low-slung tobacco-brown cars. Their antennae waved around, just as mine did, picking up scents, feeling vibrations.

And then, quite suddenly, it happened. The door of the dressing room opened. A shape so tall, it might as well have been a skyscraper, came into the room.

<We have company,> Marco announced. As if we hadn't noticed. As if our little roach brains weren't screaming at us, "Run! Run! Run!"

Then, I heard a soft snap.

The mirror on the back wall of the dressing room swung open. I felt an assault of damp air, rich with a mineral scent. I had smelled that aroma before.

Memories came rushing into my head. Memories I wished I could forget.

<Let's go!> Jake yelled.

We tore down the wall, hit the carpet, and blazed for the doorway. The feet of the Controller were just ahead of us, monstrous building-sized shoes that lifted and swung ahead, disappearing from sight.

In we went after the Controller. The door closed behind us.

<We're in,> Jake said.

<Oh, goody,> Marco replied.

CHAPTER 10

Down into the Yeerk pool.

The very last place I ever wanted to go again.

The first time we went to the Yeerk pool complex, we had taken an incredibly long stairway.

This time it was more of a ramp. It wound downward at an easy angle, no worse than walking down a driveway. And to our roach bodies, which barely experienced gravity, it was like walking on level ground.

Under our scampering feet there was bare dirt, covered by footprints. We climbed in and out of depressions that seemed to be several feet deep, by our cockroach standards.

We let the Controller pull away from us, even though we could have moved as fast as he was.

No point in taking the risk of getting stepped on.

It was dark all around, with only an occasional bare electric bulb, high, high overhead like some dim sun. Still, we wanted to be careful not to be seen. My antennae were tuned in for any vibration that might be another Controller on the path.

Down, down we went, curving and twisting between rock walls.

<Ax, how are we doing on time?> Jake asked. Ax has the ability to keep perfect track of time, even without a watch. It's a very useful talent.

<Twenty-eight of your minutes have passed since Cassie and Rachel entered morph.>

<You know, Ax, they're *your* minutes now, too,> Marco said, just to make conversation. <I mean, we are all here together on good old *Earth* where we only have one type of minute.>

We had two hours total in any morph. At two hours and one minute, we would be stuck. Like Tobias. And this was one time I actually agreed with Marco. I was not interested in being a roach forever.

<Stairs up ahead,> Cassie reported. Over, down. Over, down. Over, down. Seventy-five steps.

At last we sensed that the walls were no longer hemming us in. The path had emerged into the cavern itself.

Our roach "eyes" could not see it, but I remembered the first time I had looked down on the Yeerk pool.

It was a vast underground cavern. Larger than one of those big sports domes. The stairways and paths emerged from all sides, right about where the upper tier of seats would have been in a sports dome.

In the center of the area was the pool itself, a sludgy, muddy-looking lake that seemed to seethe with the mass of Yeerk slugs in it.

But that was not the worst of it.

Two piers were built out over the lake. One was where the Controllers — human, Hork-Bajir, Taxxon, and other species — disgorged the Yeerks from their heads. Hork-Bajir guards would watch carefully as each Controller knelt at the far end of the pier and held his head down close to the surface of the lake.

The Yeerk slug would then slither out of the host's ear and drop with a flat splash into the lake.

That's when you would discover whether the Controller was a "voluntary" host, or someone who had been taken against his will.

See, the voluntary hosts — the ones who had *chosen* to turn themselves over to the Yeerks — would stand up and calmly walk away.

The involuntary hosts would realize that they were temporarily free of the evil alien in their heads. That they once more had control over their own minds and bodies. Some would scream. Some would cry. Many would beg to be released.

A few would try to escape. But the Hork-Bajir were there to grab them and haul them to cages. That's where they would await the moment when they would be taken to the second pier.

The second pier was the place where Yeerks, now strong from their swim in the pool and full of the nutrition of Kandrona rays, would slither back inside their hosts.

When I had nightmares about the Yeerk pool . . . and I had those nightmares a lot . . . it would always be about that second pier.

The voluntary hosts would kneel and receive the Yeerks back into their brains.

The involuntaries would struggle. They would fight. Curse. Some would dare the Hork-Bajir to kill them.

We were on a ramp again. No one had said anything for a while as we still raced lower and lower, deeper and deeper, closer and closer.

That memory was in all of our minds. All except Ax, who had not been there.

<I wish I could see more clearly,> Ax said. <I wish I could see all that is going on.>

<No. You don't,> I told him.

CHAPTER 11

 e were at the end of the ramp. We reached the flat floor of the cavern.

<Okay, now what?> Cassie wondered. <We've used up at least three-quarters of an hour.>

<Forty-one of your minutes,> Ax said.

<Okay,> Jake said. <You guys remember there were buildings all around the edge of the cavern, set back from the Yeerk pool? Most are probably storage. Some may be generators and air purifiers. But some may be offices, control rooms, or even hold the Kandrona itself. We need to check out some of those buildings.>

<Well, that's what bugs do best,> Marco joked.

<I wish we could have found a bug morph with better eyes,> I said. <How are we going to even find these buildings? I can't see more than a couple of feet in front of me.>

<Don't need to,> Cassie said. <We can smell. They have humans down here. I don't know about Hork-Bajir and Taxxons, but if there are humans down here, they must eat somewhere. And I swear I smell french fries.>

She was right. I don't know if they were fries, but my roach brain definitely detected food.

<Go for the fries!> Jake said with a laugh.

We barreled away across the dusty ground. Just ahead, a wall loomed. It was easy enough to find a crack. A roach can slide through a crack no thicker than a quarter.

We emerged into brilliant light and an assault of sounds and smells.

<So. Where do you think we are?> Marco asked.

<This looks like linoleum under us,> I said. <Dirty linoleum. I feel a lot of vibrations—lots of feet, I'm guessing. And voices. Too many for me to make sense of them.>

<I smell humans,> Ax confirmed.

<Humans don't smell,> I said, only half-joking.

<Oh, humans smell,> Ax argued. <It's not a *bad* smell. Sort of like an animal we have back on my planet called a *flaar*.>

<So we have french fries and humans,> Marco said. <Are you telling me we have reached the Yeerk pool McDonald's?>

<If it's some kind of lunchroom or something, it would be a good place to listen in on conversations,> Cassie said. <Maybe we can get closer. Crawl up under a table. We should be able to——>

Suddenly a shadow fell over us. Something huge was overhead, blocking out the harsh fluorescent light.

<Now, *that* . . . that is not a human smell,> Ax said.

<I smell it, too,> I said. <It's familiar. I don't like it. Something . . . I've smelled it before . . . it's . . . I can't get my human memory and my roach senses together. It smells like . . .>

<Taxxon!> Cassie said suddenly. <Look. That tree-looking thing up there. I think it's a Taxxon leg!>

<Oh, gross. I *hate* those things,> I said.

<LOOK OUT!>

Hurtling down from the fluorescent sky at incredible speed came something like a bright red whip.

I powered my six legs in instant response.

It was too fast!

The red whip slapped the ground all around me. It fell over me like an awful, wet quilt. Something like glue oozed around me, seeping under my shell, gumming up my legs.

<Nooo!> I screamed.

<I'm trapped!> Marco cried.

I was lifted up off the ground. My back was glued to the red whip, and I was hurtling through space. I caught a wild glimpse of the others, stuck to the red whip just like me.

<What's happening?!> Cassie cried.

<It's the Taxxon,> Ax said. <I think he's about to consume us!>

We were stuck to the froglike tongue of the Taxxon, as the evil creature slurped his tongue back down his throat.

<I can't get loose!> Jake yelled. In an instant, without warning, death had come for us. I was glued down, helpless, as the Taxxon's red tongue sucked back into its mouth.

And then . . .

And then . . . everything, everywhere, stopped.

CHAPTER 12

The sticky red whip of the Taxxon's tongue stopped moving.

But it was more than that. Nothing was vibrating against my antennae. There were no sounds. There were no smells, because the air itself had stopped moving.

Then, without meaning to, I began to demorph.

<What's going on?> I asked.

<I'm demorphing,> Cassie said. <But it wasn't me doing it.>

<Are we dead? Is this some kind of hallucination?> I asked.

<If it is, I'm having it, too,> Jake said.

I swiftly grew larger and larger. My center pair of cockroach legs dwindled and disappeared. My lower legs swelled and grew skin.

I fell from the Taxxon's tongue to the ground, too large and heavy to be stuck any longer.

Toes appeared. Fingers appeared. My true human eyes opened.

I looked around, dazed and disoriented.

The others were all there. We were all human again, barefoot and dressed in our skintight morphing outfits, like we always were when we came out of a morph.

Ax was back in his Andalite body, just adding to the general weirdness of the scene.

We were inside a building. As we had guessed, it was a lunchroom. There was a kitchen to one side. There were a dozen long tables down the middle of the room.

People sat at the tables, eating. Only . . . they weren't eating. They were holding forks. They were looking down at plates of food. They were getting ready to speak. They were holding mugs of coffee.

But no one was moving.

No one was breathing.

The steam rising from the mugs of coffee was frozen and still as a photograph.

"Okay. I'm ready to wake up now," Marco said. "This dream is getting weird."

"Look," I said. "Hork-Bajir."

Two Hork-Bajir were standing by the door. I had never seen one standing still before. Even frozen in place they were frightening — seven feet of knife-edged arms, legs, head, and tail. SaladShooters on legs, as Marco said. Walking razor blades.

And then there was the Taxxon. The one who had been about to eat us. It was a monstrously big centipede, as big around as a concrete sewer pipe. It had a round, red mouth at the very top of its worm body. The long, red whip of a tongue stuck out and hung in the air.

"I have an idea," Marco said. "Even if this is a dream . . . let's get OUT of here!"

"Definitely," I agreed.

"MOVE!" Jake said loudly.

We ran for the door of the lunchroom. Out into the vast, intimidating openness of the cavern.

Outside, the same freeze had occurred. The surface of the Yeerk pool was still. The humans and Hork-Bajir who were involuntary hosts were frozen in their cages, screaming and crying and shouting without a sound or a movement.

On the infestation pier, a woman was bent low over the water, held down by a Hork-Bajir. A Yeerk was halfway into her ear. She was crying. Her tears were motionless on her cheeks.

Then I saw something moving. One single thing in all that eerie stillness.

A boy. He was tall, a little gangly. He had hair that looked as if it had never been combed.

"Oh . . ." I whispered. "Oh . . . look! It's Tobias!"

The others all turned to see.

Tobias shrugged his human shoulders. He held up his hands to stare at his own fingers. "It is me," he said, sounding like he doubted it. "My old body. Here."

I ran to him. I don't really know why, I just did. I wanted to touch him. To know he was real.

"Ah! Ah! Ah!" he yelled. He jumped back and suddenly threw his arms up and down.

He was flapping, trying to get away. Trying to fly. I had scared him by rushing at him.

"Sorry," he whispered, terribly embarrassed. "Sorry."

I put my arms around him and hugged him tightly.

"Tobias, what's going on?" I asked him.

"I don't know," he said. "I was flying . . . then suddenly, I was here. Like this."

<Time has stopped,> Ax said. <For everyone but us. I can feel it.>

"Something is very, very wrong," Cassie said darkly. "Is this some trick of Visser Three's?"

<This is not Yeerk technology, I can tell you that,> Ax said. <This is far beyond them. Far beyond us Andalites, as well.>

WHAT? HUMILITY? FROM AN ANDALITE?

"Yaaahhh!" Marco screamed.

The voice came from everywhere at once. And from nowhere. It wasn't a voice, not really. It wasn't even thought-speak. It was like an idea that simply popped into your head. The words exploded like bursting balloons inside your own thoughts.

I spun around, looking for the source, ready to fight if necessary.

NO, RACHEL. THERE IS NO THREAT.

"It knows your name!" Tobias hissed.

I glanced at Ax. He had gone rigid. He wasn't frozen like all the world around us, he was afraid. He was shaking.

AXIMILI-ESGARROUTH-ISTHILL HAS BEGUN TO GUESS WHAT I AM.

<Ellimist!> Ax said.

DO NOT BE AFRAID. I WILL APPEAR IN A PHYSICAL FORM YOU CAN UNDERSTAND.

The air directly in front of me . . . no, not in front, behind. Beside. Around. I can't explain it. The air just opened up. As if there were a door in nothingness. As if air were solid and . . . it is just impossible to explain.

The air opened. He appeared.

He was humanoid. Two arms, two legs, a head where a human head would be.

His skin was glowing blue, as if he were a light-bulb that had been painted over so that light still shone from him.

He seemed like an old man, but with a force of energy that was definitely not frail. His hair was long and white. His ears were swept up into points. His eyes were black holes that seemed to be full of stars.

"I am an Ellimist," he said, speaking with an actual voice, "as your Andalite friend guessed."

Ax was shaking so badly he looked like he might fall down.

"Be at peace, Andalite," the Ellimist said. "Look at your human friends. They do not fear me."

<They don't know what you are,> Ax managed to say.

The Ellimist smiled. "Neither do you. All you know are the fairy stories your people tell to children."

"Well, how about if someone tells us who and what you are?" I said. I was not in the best mood ever. It was extremely bizarre and unnerving to be surrounded by Human-Controllers, Hork-Bajir, and Taxxons, in the very heart of the enemy's stronghold. They were all frozen, but that could change.

To be honest, I was scared. And when I'm scared, I get mad.

The Ellimist looked at me. "You cannot begin to understand what I am."

<They are all-powerful,> Ax said simply. <They can cross a million light-years in a single instant. They can make entire worlds disappear. They can stop time itself.>

"This one doesn't look all that powerful," Marco said skeptically.

<Don't be a fool,> Ax snapped. <That's not his body. He has no body. He is . . . everywhere at once. Inside your head. Inside this planet. Inside the fabric of space and time.>

"So why are you here?" Jake asked the Ellimist. "Why all of this? Why did you bring Tobias here?"

"Obviously, you saw right through our morphs," Marco said. "You knew who we were. You even know our names. You brought us all here together. Why?"

"Because you must decide," the Ellimist said.

"Decide what?" I demanded.

"The fate of your race," the Ellimist said. "The fate of the human race."

CHAPTER 13

T hat's all?" Marco asked. "Just the fate of the human race? Don't you have something more challenging for us?"

But the Ellimist wasn't paying attention to Marco. "We do not interfere in the private affairs of other beings," he said. "But when they are in danger of becoming extinct, we step in to save a few members. We love life. All life, but especially sentient life forms, like *Homo sapiens*. Your species. This is a very beautiful planet. A priceless work of art."

"You've obviously never seen our school," Marco said, still giddily trying to joke.

Suddenly, without warning, the Ellimist did it again. He opened space.

We were no longer standing in the Yeerk pool. We were no longer underground at all.

We were underwater.

Deep underwater. But the water did not seem to touch my skin. And when I breathed, there was air. Still, I felt fear tingle the back of my neck.

We stood — me, Cassie, Jake, Marco, Ax, and Tobias . . . Tobias, in his own human body — in the middle of an ocean. Suspended in the water, but dry. The Ellimist could no longer be seen.

We were floating above a coral reef. And everything was moving again.

All around us, fish swam by in swift-darting schools. Fish in every color and shape, reflecting the dappled sunlight from above. Sharks prowled. Stingrays seemed to fly. Squid pulsated. Crabs scuttled across fabulous extrusions of coral. Tuna as big as sheep drifted past. Swift, grinning dolphins raced by in pursuit of their next meal.

LOVELY.

The Ellimist's voice once more seemed to grow from deep within my own heart.

LOVELY.

And then, as quickly as we had been plunged into the ocean, we were drifting above the waving

74

golden grass of the African savannah. A pride of lions lazed in the sun below us, looking sleepily content. Wildebeest and gazelles and impalas grazed, then broke into wild, springing, bouncing races that forced you to smile at the sheer energy of it all.

There were hyenas, rhinos, elephants, giraffes, cheetahs, baboons, zebras. Hawks and eagles and buzzards wheeled overhead.

LOOK AT IT.

Then, in an instant, deep jungle. A lithe jaguar prowled while monkeys chattered in the tree canopy above. Snakes as long as a person slithered across tree branches. The air reeked of the heavy perfume of a million flowers. We heard the sounds of frogs, insects, monkeys, and wild, screaming birds.

IN ALL THE UNIVERSE, NO GREATER BEAUTY.

IN A THOUSAND, THOUSAND WORLDS, NO GREATER ART THAN THIS.

Then the Ellimist showed us the human race.

We flew, invisible, through the steel-and-glass canyons of New York City.

We drifted above villages at the edges of jungle rivers. We watched a rock concert in Rio de Janeiro, and a political meeting in Seoul, and a soccer game in Durban, and an open-air market in the Philippines.

HUMANS. CRUDE. PRIMITIVE. BUT CAPABLE OF UNDERSTANDING.

Suddenly all the movement stopped. We were

staring at a picture. A painting. I'd seen the painting somewhere before.

It was a wild swirl of color. A painting of purple flowers. Irises, I think, although I'm no big expert on flowers. The artist had seen the beauty of those flowers and captured some small bit of it on canvas.

CAPABLE OF UNDERSTANDING.

Then, without warning, we were back in the Yeerk pool.

The images were all gone. We were in the land of despair once again. Surrounded by frozen images of horror.

The Ellimist—or at least the body he had made for us to look at—reappeared.

"That was a nice tour," I said. I was trying to sound tough. But I felt as if I had been turned inside out. As if my mind had exploded into a thousand sparkling pieces. I was overwhelmed. "But what's it all about?"

"Humans are an endangered species. Soon you will disappear."

I thought of a couple things to say. But I said nothing. No one said anything.

"The Yeerk race is also sentient," the Ellimist said. "And they are technologically more advanced than you. They will continue to infest the human race. The Andalites will try to stop them, but they will fail.

The Yeerks will win. And soon, the only humans left will be what you call Human-Controllers."

I had stopped breathing. The way he said it . . . it was like you couldn't argue. Like you couldn't say anything. He spoke every word with utter and complete certainty.

He wasn't guessing. He *knew*.

He knew that we would lose.

CHAPTER 14

I had been terrified a few moments before, as the Taxxon prepared to swallow us. I had been afraid for my own life and the lives of my friends.

Now, as the Yeerk pool hung suspended in time, I felt a deeper fear. My head was still swimming from all the images the Ellimist had shown us.

"Why come here just to tell us we're dead meat?" I managed to ask.

"We have an offer for you," the Ellimist said. "You see, we can save a small sample of the human race. We have a planet where we would relocate you. You . . . some members of your family. A few others, chosen to get a good genetic sampling. As well as a few non-human Earth species that are of special interest to us."

I was surprised to hear Cassie actually laugh. "He's some kind of environmentalist," she said. "That's what he is. We're the spotted owls. We're the rhinos. We're the whales. We're the endangered species, and he's the environmentalist trying to save us."

"We have a planet set aside for you," the Ellimist said. "It will seem very much like Earth. You would be free to evolve naturally, as your species should."

"This is insane," Marco said. "It's like Noah's ark. The Yeerk flood is coming. Load up the boat."

"No," Tobias said, staring at the Ellimist. "It's a zoo. That's what he has for us — a zoo."

The Ellimist said, "We do not impose our will on sentient species. The decision is yours. I have chosen you to decide, because only you, of all free humans, know what is happening. You must decide — to stay on Earth and fight a battle you are certain to lose. Or to leave this planet behind and form part of a new colony of humans."

"How long do we have to decide?" Jake asked.

"You must decide now," the Ellimist said.

"What?" I yelled. "What? What are you up to? What do you mean, we have to decide *now*?"

This was beyond insane. This was a dream. This couldn't even be real. I was imagining it all.

"If you decide the answer is yes, you, and some of those you are close to, will be instantly taken to your new home. If the answer is no, I will return everything to the way it was when I interrupted time."

"You mean we're back in roach morph headed down that Taxxon's throat?" I asked.

"Everything as it was," the Ellimist said. "Our purpose is not to interfere."

I looked at Tobias. His face showed nothing. Maybe he had forgotten how to show emotion.

"And our friend Tobias?" Cassie asked softly.

"*Everything* as it was," the Ellimist repeated.

"Oh, that's real fair," Marco said. "You ask us this just as we're about to be some Taxxon's lunch?"

"This is ridiculous," Jake said angrily. "You can't just tell us we have to make a decision like this. We are not the ones who should be deciding this. I mean, maybe you're trying to do the right thing for us, but this is nuts."

<Ellimists are not interested in what is fair,> Ax said. <Ellimists give you a choice that is no choice at all. Then they can claim that they do not interfere. They will *pretend* it was a human decision.>

It was hard to argue with Ax's opinion. The Ellimist had totally rigged this decision. Realizing that made me want to resist. The Ellimist wanted us to say yes. He wanted us to abandon the fight against the Yeerks.

And yet . . . a place where we would have peace. A place where the fighting would be over. Where we could be normal kids. No more decisions. No more battles.

The Ellimist had said we would be with some of the people we were close to. Who? Who would be saved?

"I vote no," Tobias said, with sharp, angry defiance. "You're using me. You're using my friends' affection for me as a tool. And I'm not going for it."

"Let's think this over a little first, Tobias," Cassie pleaded. "I mean, just because we're upset . . . this decision is for the whole human race. Do you understand that? He's talking about humanity becoming *extinct*."

"Tobias, you personally have a lot to lose," Jake reminded him. "If we say no, you're right back in your hawk body."

"So we have two votes no, Tobias and Rachel, one vote yes from Cassie," Marco said.

But I *hadn't* voted. Marco had just assumed. . . . And he was right, I realized with a sick churning in my stomach. Marco was right about me. I had to vote no. If Tobias was ready to stay in the fight, with all he had to lose, I couldn't do less.

"What this character wants us to do is run away," I said. "He wants us to abandon our people and our planet just to save ourselves and the people we care about personally."

Tobias met my gaze. There appeared a faint flicker of his old, human smile.

<This is a decision for humans,> Ax said. <I fight the Yeerks. I follow Prince Jake. But I don't trust this Ellimist, however great his power.>

"Guys, I know how you feel," Cassie said, "but *think* about this. We may not even get out of this Yeerk pool alive. And if we die, then what chance do humans have against the Yeerks? And anyway, he says that humans will lose. Isn't it better to save *some* humans, rather than losing *everyone*?"

Jake and Marco had still not voted. I noticed that they were looking back toward the building we had come from. And past the building, to what looked like a tall, circular column rising straight up to the rock ceiling of the cavern.

The column was a mix of steel and clear glass. Inside the column was a Human-Controller, seemingly frozen in midair. She looked like she had been falling down the long tube.

Or else flying up it.

A dropshaft! We had used one aboard the Yeerk mother ship. It was a sort of elevator that worked on some invisible force to let you fall safely from one level to another.

But did it go *up*, as well as *down*? That was the question. Was the Human-Controller in the shaft falling or rising?

Jake cocked an eyebrow at me. He looked back to the column, making sure I had noticed it.

I squinted closely at the frozen Controller. She had shoulder-length hair. If she were falling, it should have been swept upward. It was down around her neck.

"Mr. Ellimist," Marco said, "thanks for your offer. But I don't think so. I don't think I want to be in your zoo. And I don't like being muscled like this. I'm glad you like Earth, but we'll take care of it the best way we can."

That made it four against. Me, Marco, Tobias, and Ax. I counted Ax, even if he said it wasn't up to him.

Cassie was alone in leaning in favor of the Ellimist's offer.

"You all know I take care of lots of sick animals. They are always afraid of me, even though I am trying to help them. Are we being brave saying no? Or are we just being foolish, resisting someone who is trying to save us?"

What she said made me think. With a shock, I pictured nature films I had seen. I remembered one that showed environmentalists attempting to capture some tigers. They were trying to move the tigers to a game preserve where they would be safe. Tigers are almost extinct, and the humans were trying to save a few.

But the tigers had resisted. They had growled and fought and avoided the capture nets.

Was that us? Were we animals on the edge of extinction, resisting the being who'd come to save us?

I wondered if I should change my vote. Save myself. Save my family. What would they say, if *they* had a vote? My mom? She would never risk the lives of her children. She would vote yes.

And my dad? If we were all magically transported to a safe place together, and I had to explain what I had done? That I had voted to save all of us and give up the fight? What would he think of that decision?

"You know what bothers me?" I heard Jake tell the Ellimist. "You say the human race will lose to the Yeerks. But I don't believe you can tell the future. See, you don't know how we're going to vote. If you did, you wouldn't bother to be here, would you?" He looked around at each of us.

Cassie smiled sadly. "If you guys vote to stay, I will, too."

Jake reached out and took her hand. "Mr. Ellimist, I guess you have your an—"

CHAPTER 15

—Swer.>

Instantly, we were back in our roach bodies.

IF YOU LIVE, I WILL ASK ONCE MORE.

IF YOU LIVE.

The red whip of the Taxxon's tongue held me glued down, helpless!

<Morph! Morph out!> Jake yelled in my head.

I didn't need to be told twice.

Through the fear, I focused my mind on my own human body. Suddenly everything around me went dark.

<We're inside the Taxxon!> I yelled.

<Focus on morphing!> Jake yelled. <We are busting out of here.>

A gush of stinging liquid, like a tidal wave, washed me from the sticky tongue. I tumbled blind and terrified through hot, viscous goo.

But at the same time I could feel that I was growing. My roach antennae brushed against something very close to me. Another cockroach. But bigger than it should have been.

<Demorphing!> Cassie yelled.

<Right with you,> I yelled back.

Everything was closing in around me. The bodies of the others were shoved against mine as we all grew out of our roach morphs. I felt the gut of the Taxxon spasming as it tried to deal with this deadly growing meal.

My human lungs were growing back, and as they grew they began to need air.

I was suffocating! My body was not as durable as the roach form.

<Air!> I heard Marco cry. <I can't breathe.>

<Just keep morphing,> Jake said. <We'll try and pop this worm open.>

<I have my tail again,> Ax said. <Should I—>

<YES!> Jake said. <Do it!>

The darkness around us split open suddenly. I caught a glimpse of Ax's scythelike Andalite tail slicing the Taxxon open from the inside.

Air! Air rushed in. Stinking, foul, vile air, but air.

We exploded from the inside of the Taxxon, wrapped in its guts, covered with green-blue slime.

We were not fully human yet, still some awful melding of human and bug, but we were finishing our demorphing as fast as we ever had.

Air! I sucked it into my still-forming lungs.

The Taxxon lay ruined and reeking all around us. The room full of Human-Controllers eating dinner was no longer frozen by the Ellimist.

Now they were frozen by sheer disbelief.

"Let's bail!" I yelled. "Before they can think about it."

We ran. Slipping and slithering through the Taxxon's guts, still forming the last of our fingers and toes, we tore out of there.

"Get them!" a human voice yelled. "Get them, you fools, or Visser Three will chew your bones!"

Suddenly, with a roar, the Human-Controllers surged up out of their chairs.

A Hork-Bajir near the door moved swiftly to cut us off. Ax swung his tail with blinding speed. It hit the Hork-Bajir in his shoulder.

"Head for the dropshaft!" Marco cried as he led the way from the room.

"Everyone but Ax, if you can morph again, *do* it!"

Jake yelled as we raced for the dropshaft. "We need firepower!"

I didn't need to be told. The only one of us who had any kind of natural ability to fight was Ax. I was already trying to focus my mind on the bear that I had made a part of me.

Part of me knew it was foolish. I should morph the elephant, or a wolf. I knew both of those morphs; I could handle them. But I also knew the elephant might not fit in the dropshaft. And I wanted power.

Whumpf!

Something hit me and I went sprawling across the dirt.

A man stood over me. A grown man! He had slammed into me. For some reason, this outraged me. What kind of a creep would hit a girl half his size?

Of course I knew the answer. I knew the man was not really a man at all, but a Controller. The Yeerk in his head didn't care about chivalry.

The man bent over me and began to put his hands around my throat.

Suddenly he only had one hand.

"Aaarrrgghhh!" he cried, falling back.

"Thanks, Ax," I said.

<We are trapped,> he said.

I looked past him. The others had all reached the dropshaft, a hundred feet away. Between the two of us and them was a small army of Human-Controllers and Hork-Bajir.

As I watched, Marco, and then Cassie, were swept up the dropshaft. Only Jake was still standing there. He looked back at us with an expression of horror.

"Jake, get OUT of here!" I screamed. "We'll be okay!"

Several of the Controllers began closing in on Jake. But most of them only had eyes for Ax. They could see that he was an Andalite—the deadly enemy of all Yeerks. I don't know what they thought I was, still dripping with Taxxon goo.

Suddenly a pair of Hork-Bajir warriors rushed at us. Their bladed arms slashed the air. They came at us like a pair of chainsaws on high speed.

Ax struck!

But the Hork-Bajir were too fast.

<Aaaarrrhh!>

There was a deep gash down Ax's flank.

He struck again and again, his scorpion tail almost invisible. The Human-Controllers stayed prudently back, as much afraid of getting sliced and diced by the angry Hork-Bajir as by Ax. But more Hork-Bajir were rushing up, and Ax was losing ground.

Then . . . I realized I was no longer afraid.

A deep confidence had welled up inside of me.

Utter confidence. Utter fearlessness.

I realized I was no longer standing erect. I was on all fours. When I looked down I expected to see my two hands splayed on the dirt. Instead I saw massive paws.

Coarse, dark brown fur. Black claws, each like the point of a pickax.

I had become the bear. It was *his* confidence I felt. It was *his* total lack of fear.

I was an animal that had never, in a thousand generations of grizzly bears, known an instant of real fear.

Suddenly I felt a terrible pain in my shoulder. One of the Hork-Bajir had slashed me. I glared with near-sighted eyes and saw nothing but a tall blur.

I had never morphed the bear before. I had never learned to control its brain, its instincts. The bear mind was focused completely on one basic fact—it had been challenged.

There was exactly one response to being challenged.

Attack!

"Grrooowwwrrrr!" I roared. I charged the Hork-Bajir.

He cut me again. It didn't matter. I barreled into him, eight hundred pounds of very angry grizzly.

The power!

I was a truck doing seventy miles an hour!

I was a tank!

I was the largest carnivore on land and nothing, NOTHING challenged me and survived!

I could barely see the Hork-Bajir through the bear's weak eyes, but I smelled him and felt him, and I swung my massive paw and hit him full in the chest. I struck him with a blow that would have knocked a train off its tracks.

The Hork-Bajir went flying.

More came.

More discovered why part of the Latin name for the grizzly is *horribilis*.

I barely remember what happened next. I gave myself up to the bear's rage. Its anger and my own became one. All the tension within me, all the uncertainty, all the doubts were swept away as I gave myself up to the bear's violence.

I remember that at some point, Jake got into his tiger morph and joined the fight. And I have flashing images from my memory of terrible destruction. Of ripping claws and crushing jaws.

But the next thing I clearly remember is flying up the long dropshaft, while Jake's voice in my head kept saying, <Rachel, morph out. Morph out. You're out of control! You are OUT of control! Morph!>

I was clawing wildly at the air, trying to kill the tiger that was suspended above me in the dropshaft.

Trying to kill Jake.

I felt as if I had snapped awake from a dream.

Slowly, as we rose toward the surface, I left the bear and returned to myself.

CHAPTER 16

The soaring rush up the dropshaft seemed to last forever.

The dropshaft entered solid rock, and as I rose, I shed the last of my bear form. I felt the return of my human reason. But I was still confused and disconnected from what was going on.

Then, quite suddenly, I was at the top of the dropshaft. I stepped off onto solid concrete. The others were all there. Ax was trying to morph into his human body, but he was having trouble. Morphing is exhausting. Morphing rapidly from one form to the next more than once makes you feel like you want to just crawl in a corner and die.

I knew how he felt. I stumbled from sheer weariness as I stepped onto the cement floor. It was dark, with just enough faint light to see the faces around me.

"Careful," Cassie said, taking my arm. "We're okay. We're safe. We're in the base of the water tower behind the school."

"Gotta get out of here. Yeerks will be watching."

"Yeah, they were," Marco said. He jerked his head over to the corner, where two Human-Controllers lay unconscious.

"Let's get out of here," Jake said. "You okay, Rachel?"

"Yeah. Tired is all. I . . . I never morphed the bear before. Didn't have time to get control. Sorry."

"It's okay, Rachel. That grizzly got us all out of there. But get some rest, huh?"

"Yeah. Rest would be nice."

Somehow I made it home. I crawled into my bed and fell instantly asleep.

I didn't wake up till the next morning when my alarm went off. I was groggy, barely able to read the numbers on my clock.

"Rachel? Are you up?" my mom called through the door.

"Yeah. Yeah, I'm up," I said.

I crawled out of bed and staggered toward the bathroom. Jordan was in the bathroom we share. I went out into the hall toward my mother's bathroom.

She was already up and dressed in a tan business suit. She was adjusting her nylons. "You don't look too good," she said, giving me a sideways look.

"Uh," I said. "Can I use your shower?"

"You're wearing the clothes you came home in last night," she said accusingly. "You came wandering in at nine thirty, barefoot and wearing your leotard. That's what you're still wearing."

I stared stupidly down at myself. Yes, I was wearing my morphing outfit. "Um . . . my, um, I left my shoes over at Cassie's. I was showing her some gymnastics stuff. Can I use your shower or not?"

"Coming home barefoot and falling asleep without even having dinner," my mom said, and shook her head. "Rachel, if you are having some problems or something, I want you to talk to me."

I did the wrong thing: I suddenly burst out laughing. "Problems? No, why would I have any problems?" I giggled, and wiped the sleep from my eyes, and giggled some more.

My mom sighed. "I have an early court appearance this morning," she said. "The Hallinan case. But I want you to stay home tonight. I think you and I need to have a little talk. I know your father has thrown a big problem into your lap. I know this decision is very difficult for you."

"Can I use your shower or not?" I sighed, no longer giggling.

"Go ahead. Make sure Sara gets on the bus okay."

I closed the bathroom door behind me and fled to the sanctuary of steaming hot water.

It started coming back to me then. All of it. Exploding out of the Taxxon's stomach. The Ellimist's offer. The sight of Tobias, back for too brief a time in his own body. Human again.

And the battle . . . a rampaging, enraged bear. A bear that was me.

I shuddered. I was running out of hot water.

"Rachel? What did you do, fall in?" It was Jordan, outside the bathroom door.

"Jordan? Make sure Sara gets off to school, okay?" I called out. "I'm running a little late. You go ahead, too."

I skipped school that day for the first time in my life. I lay around the house and watched daytime trash TV. I flipped channels back and forth, between one bunch of messed-up people and another bunch of even more messed-up people.

It was nice, watching other people with problems. Their problems all seemed easy compared to mine.

But over the electronic pictures of angry people and placating hosts, other images appeared. A Taxxon, split open like a torn bag of garbage. The frozen, silent screams of involuntary hosts in their cages.

And through all the television noise, I could still hear other voices. The Ellimist's voice in my head. *We can save a small sample of the human race.*

And Jake's voice. *You are out of control!*

And my father. *To another city. Another state.*

I tried not to even think about everything that had happened the day before. I mean, it was so ridiculous. I lived in two completely different worlds.

One world was filled by my family, school, gymnastics classes, shopping, listening to music, watching TV . . . normal stuff.

But then I had this whole other life. A life where I wasn't just Jordan and Sara's big sister, and my mom's first child, and a teacher's pet, and a gymnastics student who was weak on the balance beam.

In my other life I was . . . a warrior. I risked my life. I fought in deadly nightmare battles against terrible odds. I became so much more than just a kid.

Noon rolled around and I made myself a grilled cheese sandwich. I turned on the TV in the kitchen while I cooked. And there was my dad on the noon news. He was doing a remote—a story from outside the studio. Some stupid event at the convention center.

I muted the sound and just watched the picture. I threw my sandwich in the trash.

"What am I supposed to do?!" I yelled suddenly, shocking myself. "What am I supposed to *do*?"

My voice sounded flat and dead in the silence of the kitchen. I felt foolish. It wasn't like me to get all emotional.

I stood there, just staring at the cupboards. The Ellimist . . . the bear . . . my father . . . What was I supposed to do? Leave my mom and sisters? Leave my dad? Leave my friends? Leave the whole messed-up planet?

I imagined going to see my father down at the convention center. "Dad? I have this problem." And he would put his arm around me and fluff my hair the way he always did and say, "Come on, kid. Don't be so serious."

I turned the TV sound back on. My dad was grinning at something. He was doing some chatter with the anchor people back at the station.

". . . be leaving us soon, and we're all sorry to hear that. But I know it will be a great opportunity for you."

"Yes, it will," my father said. "Although I will really miss all the—"

I snapped off the TV set. I felt sick inside. Like I had swallowed broken glass.

I needed to get out of the house. I needed to stop thinking.

I went upstairs and opened my bedroom window.

Several minutes later, a large bald eagle flew from my window and soared high into the sky.

CHAPTER 17

We all met up later that afternoon at Cassie's barn.

Inside her barn there are rows of cages in all shapes and sizes, mostly full. Birds are in one area, with mammals separated from them by a partition wall. I guess it makes the birds nervous to be in the same room with foxes and raccoons. Nervous birds hurt themselves, banging around the cages.

When I showed up at the meeting barefoot and in my morphing outfit, everyone immediately knew I hadn't exactly taken the bus to get there.

Jake and Marco were lolling on bales of hay.

Tobias was perched on a crossbeam a few feet

over our heads. I felt a stab of pain, seeing him that way again.

Ax did not come to these meetings, usually. He would have had to assume his human morph, and he preferred to remain in Andalite form as much as possible.

"Hi, Rachel," Marco said, looking amused, but also a little wary. "What have you been up to? Or maybe I should ask, what have you *been*?"

Cassie was busy changing the bandage on the wing of a sad-looking kestrel.

"Hey, Rachel," Cassie said. "Give me a hand here, will you? I didn't see you at school today."

I went and held the struggling bird as well as I could. Kestrels are small falcons. This kestrel tried to take a bite out of me, but he was too weak to do any damage.

"I felt kind of sick this morning," I told Cassie. "So I stayed home."

"But you felt better this afternoon, huh?" Jake said. "So much better that you decided to morph? How did you get here, just out of curiosity?"

Cassie was done and took the kestrel from me. I turned to look Jake in the eye. "I flew. Is that okay with you?"

He glanced at Cassie. Then at Marco. "That bear you morphed yesterday . . . you went to The Gardens and acquired that all on your own, didn't you?"

"No," I said, "I met that bear at the mall."

"Okay," Jake said. "And today you ditch school and end up morphing . . . whatever you morphed."

<An eagle,> Tobias said. <I saw a bald eagle riding the thermals this afternoon. I should have guessed. It was up for too long, acting like a buzzard. A real eagle would have perched after a while.>

"It's so nice knowing I have privacy," I said sarcastically.

<That was about noon,> Tobias said. <If you came here in eagle morph, that would be more than two hours. You must have demorphed, then morphed again.>

Jake looked at me sharply. "You spent the whole afternoon in morph?"

"Yes, *Mother*," I said.

Jake jumped up and stood right in front of me, his face just inches from mine. "Don't give me your sarcasm, Rachel. You are acting really weird. That's everyone's business, because if you do something stupid, we could all end up paying the price. You go and acquire a grizzly? Without backup? You could have been killed."

"So what?" I shot back. "You heard the Ellimist. We're doomed. It's going to be Yeerks one, humans zero. We lose. So who cares about anything? Who cares if I skip school to go flying?"

Suddenly Jake just sagged. "I don't know, Rachel. I don't have any answers. I'm sick of trying to have answers. You decide. I don't want to argue with you. I don't know what your problem is, but you know what? *You* deal with it."

I've never seen Jake look so tired. One minute he was being strong, sensible Jake, leader of the Animorphs. And the next minute he looked exhausted. His eyes were red. He was blinking constantly. He looked like he was worn out just from breathing.

"My dad wants me to move out of state with him," I said.

Everyone just kind of stared at me. They all had blank, tired eyes, not much different from Jake's.

"What are you going to do?" Cassie asked.

I threw up my hands. "How can I even think about something that unimportant? I mean, like we don't have bigger things to worry about? The fate of planet Earth and the human race?"

"Different things bother different people," Cassie said. "I know how you feel about your dad."

"He's a jerk for dumping this on me!" I said loudly. "I mean . . . you know . . . I mean . . ."

It was weird. All of a sudden I felt like I was choking. Like I was ready to explode. Like my brain was spinning out of control.

"It's like . . . what am I supposed to do?!" I yelled. "After what happened last night . . . after all that, I have to decide who I want to hurt—my mom or my dad? And you guys? And—"

"Come on, Rachel," Marco said kindly. "Take it easy. Come on, you're Xena—"

"NO! No, I'm not some stupid, old TV character. I'm not some comic book, Marco. I'm scared, okay?! Just like all the rest of you. I'm scared of what almost happened to me last night. I'm scared just knowing that place exists down there. I'm scared about what happens to *me*. I just wanted to run away but I didn't think I could, so I was brave because that's the way I'm supposed to be. But now everyone's going, 'Oh, just come live with me and we'll go to ball games,' and 'Hey, forget moving to another state, we have a whole other planet for you.' And the more exits I see, the more scared I get, all right?"

For a long time no one said anything.

Marco sighed heavily. "I've been thinking. I'm changing my vote. If the Ellimist asks again, I'm going to vote yes."

"*What?*" Jake demanded. "Why?"

Marco shrugged. "Rachel's losing it. If she loses it, how long are the rest of us going to last?"

"Shut up, Marco, I'm not in the mood for your jokes," I said.

"Me neither," Marco said flatly. "You know how much sleep I got last night? About an hour. Nightmares. I was a zombie in school today. I feel like . . . like my skin has all been rubbed with sandpaper. I'm jumpy. I'm scared. I'm stressed."

"It's gonna happen," Jake said.

"This was always insane, right from the start," Marco said. "A handful of kids fighting an alien invasion? Look what's happening. Tobias is trapped in a morph. Rachel is starting to use morphing to get away from her problems. The other night I woke up in bed, and I didn't know *what* I was. I didn't know if I had hands or fins or claws or talons. Maybe you and Cassie are immune, Jake. But I doubt it."

"We can't give up," Jake argued stubbornly.

"All we ever do is lose," Marco said. "We annoy the Yeerks. Maybe we blow up a ship, or have some little success. But the invasion marches on. And all we ever do is barely escape with our lives. We're like some baseball team that never wins a game. And now, according to the Ellimist, we know it's going to be a whole losing season. We aren't going to the play-offs."

"I don't care," Jake said. "I'm not giving up."

"Jake," Cassie said. "See this?" She held up her left arm and pointed to a scar above her wrist. "I got this from a raccoon. The raccoon had been caught in a trap. Its leg was broken. I was trying to free it so I could save it. It bit me."

"We're not raccoons," Jake said.

"Aren't we? Compared to the Ellimist?" Cassie said. "Isn't it just possible he's right? That what he's trying to do is save at least a part of the human race? That he's just trying to get us out of the trap and fix our broken bones?"

"Cassie's right," Marco said. "If the Ellimist wanted to hurt us, he could just destroy us. You know it as well as I do. Fine. I'm going to let him get my leg out of the trap. But I have some conditions first. There are some people going with me. But if the Ellimist can save those people along with me, then I have to say yes."

Marco looked at me. Then Jake and Cassie and Tobias all looked at me. The vote was now two against two. I was the deciding vote.

It would mean no more battles. It would mean that somewhere, wherever the Ellimist took us, there would be no job in another state for my dad. There would be no more painful decisions for me to make.

I opened my mouth. I started to speak.

I PROMISED I WOULD ASK YOU AGAIN.

"Uh-oh," Marco said.

I WILL SHOW YOU WHAT YOU NEED TO UNDERSTAND.

CHAPTER 18

I WILL SHOW YOU WHAT YOU NEED TO
UNDERSTAND.

In an instant, we were gone from the barn. The
five of us and Ax stood side by side in the middle of
an empty field of scruffy, unkempt grass. There was
a long, low, tumbledown building a hundred yards
away.

The Ellimist was nowhere to be seen. We were the
only people around: five humans and one Andalite.
Five real humans.

"Tobias!" I said.

"Yeah," he said, looking down at his hands. "This
routine again."

Jake looked angry. Cassie marveled. Marco tried to smirk nonchalantly, but wasn't succeeding. No one looked tired anymore.

Ax skittered nervously on his dainty hooves and stretched his tail, as if preparing to use it.

"The Ellimist again," I said. "Did you guys hear—"

"Yeah, we heard," Jake said. "So we get another chance to change our minds."

"Where are we?" Cassie wondered. "I mean, something about this looks familiar. But I can't quite place it."

I had the same feeling. Like this empty, dusty, blasted landscape was familiar. It was Tobias who saw it first.

"The school," he said.

"What?" I said. "No way." But he was right. I looked again and realized that I knew each of those tumbledown, destroyed buildings.

"Okay, I don't like this," Marco said. "I don't even halfway like this. I mean, normally I'm all for seeing the school blown up, but I *really* don't like this."

"When did this happen?" I wondered aloud. "I skip one day and the place burns down?"

"I don't think so," Cassie said in a strange, distracted voice. "I don't think this is something that's happened, past tense. I think we're talking future tense."

"Or just tense," Marco muttered.

I looked over at Cassie, wondering what she was talking about. She was staring intently up at the sky overhead. Then off toward the horizon.

"The sky," she said. "Have you ever seen it that color before?"

"It does seem slightly yellowish," Jake said.

"And the air. Doesn't it smell funny? And look, over there. The trees over behind the gym. They're dying."

"The Ellimist said he would show us something," I muttered. "So what's he showing us? Ax? You understand any of this?"

<There is a time distortion. I sense it. But I don't know what it means.>

"It's the future," Cassie said.

A chill crawled up my spine. I wanted to think Cassie was losing it. But I sensed the truth of what she said.

"Okaaaaay," Marco said. "So, what are we supposed to do now? Stand around here until the Ellimist comes back for us?"

Jake shrugged. "I guess we look around. The mall's just a quarter mile or so. It should be open."

So we walked. Across the scruffy field. Beneath a sky that seemed to add yellow to blue and make patches and wisps of green, unlike any sky I had ever seen. We passed the school and looked morbidly through the blast holes to see if we could recognize anything.

"YAAAAHHH!" Marco yelled.

He reeled back from one of the dark holes. I ran to look inside. It was a classroom. There was a skeleton lying crumpled across the teacher's desk.

"Oh my God," Cassie whispered. "The body was just left here."

"That's Paloma's classroom," I said. "History class."

It took a few seconds for the significance of that to sink in. The body had been left there to rot. It must have taken years for it to be reduced to nothing but bones.

"Cassie's right. We're in the future," Marco said. "But that's impossible."

<Impossible for humans,> Ax said. <But not impossible for Ellimists.>

"Oh, I get it," I said angrily. "It's a little lesson. The Ellimist is showing us what happens in the future. How cute. How clever. But how do we know this is really the future, and not just some little show he's putting on?"

"Let's try the mall," Jake said. "Although I don't have a good feeling about this."

We left the school behind us. I tried not to think

about who that skeleton might have been. Some teacher? Some student? Some person who just happened to be in the wrong place at the wrong time?

"Maybe we can check the bookstore at the mall," Marco said. "Find a *World Almanac* for whatever year this is. See who won all the Super Bowls. Then when we go back to our own time, we can bet on the games. Make a fortune."

I forced a laugh that came out like a grunt. We needed to keep our spirits up. Marco was trying.

We reached the highway. Eight lanes of concrete, dead silent. Not a car. Not a truck. Empty.

On the far side of the highway was a rusted wreck of a car. Bony white hands clutched the steering wheel. We stayed away from it.

I saw something that gleamed brightly, off to the east. It seemed to run in a straight line from the far horizon to a point much closer. I squinted to see what it was.

"Too bad we don't have your hawk eyes now," I whispered to Tobias.

"It's a tube, I think. Like a long, long glass tube. There! Something is moving down it."

<It is a conveyance of some kind,> Ax said. He had turned all four of his eyes toward it. <It seems to be a glass tube that goes on for many miles. Inside it are fast-moving platforms, like your trains. Only faster.

They are going perhaps three hundred or more of your miles per hour.>

"They're everyone's miles," Marco said. "You're on Earth, Ax. We all have the same miles."

<What about nations that use kilometers?> Ax asked smugly. <See? I am learning.>

"Some kind of very high-speed train system," Jake said. "That's why no one is on the highway."

"The question is, who built the system?" I pointed out. A few minutes later, we reached the mall. But it had changed. It had changed quite a bit.

"Oh, man," Marco said. "Look at that! Oh, man."

The mall was still standing. Even the sign that said "Sears" could still be seen. But holes, perfectly round and about six feet across, had been drilled into the sides of the four big department stores. There were six or eight holes in the JCPenney. The same with Sears. And from the holes emerged Taxxons.

They crawled in and out of the holes. They slithered down to the ground and up to the roof. Some were carrying boxes from a squat, bulky spacecraft that sat in the parking lot. They were unloading it like a truck, carrying silvery packages in through several of the holes.

"It's a hive," Cassie said. "It's like a beehive. Or an ant colony. They've taken it over. The mall is a Taxxon hive."

CHAPTER 19

The future the way it will be if the Yeerks win," I said. "Taxxons using the mall for a hive. I guess that means I can forget about any good sales today."

I wanted to sound tough. Like I wasn't impressed. But that was a lie. Worms larger than a grown man were crawling through holes in the mall. Skeletons lay across desks in the shattered ruins of our school, and clutched the wheels of rusted cars.

The air felt strange. The sky was no longer the sky of Earth. The trees were dying.

As we circled around the mall, we could see that the tube train made a stop there. The glass tube was

raised above the ground about t   e
monorail at Disney World. But   o
be enough supports to hold i   e
just hanging there.

Outside the mall, a dropsh
A Taxxon entered the shaft a
platform that bulged from the

"Let's stay clear of any Taxx

But Marco shook his head. "
The Yeerks have won. So any
Controllers. The Taxxons would
Human-Controllers."

"I guess you're right," Tobia
we can go anywhere. Besides, I d
brought us here to see us get killed."

I relaxed a little, realizing they were right. But still, there was a deeply disturbing feeling about all of it.

<I will morph into human form,> Ax said. <The Yeerks may be accustomed to Human-Controllers. But they will not have seen any Andalite-Controllers except for Visser Three.>

"Are you so sure?" Marco asked. "Maybe in the future the Andalites lose to the Yeerks, too."

<Never,> Ax snapped angrily.

He began to slowly melt into human shape.

"Let's hop the train," I said. "See where it goes."

"Excuse me?" Marco laughed. "Climb aboard the Yeerk version of Amtrak?"

I shrugged. "You said it, Marco. They'll think we're Controllers. And in any case, the Ellimist didn't bring us here to get us killed."

"It is sad about the mall," Ax said, now mostly human. "They had excellent foods for tasting. Tay-sting. Tasting. The Ellimist showed us much of what was excellent in your species and your planet. But he did not mention the sense of taste. Cinnamon buns. Buns. Bunzuh. And chocolate, too."

"Yeah, we have to save any species that can invent the warm cinnamon bun," I said. "Come on, let's try this."

It only took a couple minutes to walk to the drop-shaft. As we neared it, a Taxxon slithered up alongside us. He was racing to get ahead, like a rushing com-muter. But aside from that, he paid us no mind.

"You think the Yeerks have a rush hour?" Marco muttered under his breath.

"Quiet," Jake snapped. "We're Controllers now, not normal humans."

The Taxxon reached the dropshaft ahead of us. He stepped in through the large opening and was immediately swept up onto the platform overhead.

We all hesitated to follow him. So I stepped

forward. Seconds later I was on the platform, with the others right behind me.

We were twenty feet up, and I could see in all directions.

I nudged Tobias. A small Yeerk pool had been built on the roof of the mall. Right over the place where the food court had been. It was a shallow, sludgy pool. Half a dozen Taxxons lounged around it, almost as if they were sunbathing.

There were no cages at this Yeerk pool. Taxxons are all voluntary hosts. Another reason not to like them. At least the Hork-Bajir had resisted the Yeerks.

Suddenly, in a rush of wind, a platform came down the glass tube like a bullet.

It stopped in front of us and the Taxxon quickly slithered aboard. We followed.

It was not a closed car like a train. It was just a clear platform, open at the front end and the back. There were maybe twenty standard seats, half occupied by Human-Controllers. Toward the back was an open area where the Taxxon went. At the front were several larger chairs. Much larger, and made of steel with no padding.

Those had to be for Hork-Bajir. Space for about four Hork-Bajir, maybe two or three Taxxons, and seats for twenty or more humans.

So there were far more humans around than

either Taxxons or Hork-Bajir, I concluded. We would not look out of place.

The train launched like a bullet down the glass tunnel. But there was no lurch. And no rushing wind. We just blew along at a speed that boggled the mind.

The trip from the suburban mall to downtown usually took half an hour by bus. We made the trip in about a minute and a half.

Jake gave me a look. We were getting off here. We rose and left the train.

"Fast," Marco said.

"Beats the bus," I agreed.

It was beyond strange, walking the streets of downtown. Entire skyscrapers were simply gone. Others now had wormholes for the Taxxons. I looked up thirty stories and saw Taxxons crawling up the sides of a building that used to be the headquarters for a bank.

The tallest building in town was the EGS Tower. It was sixty stories tall. It still stood, almost intact. But for some reason the top two floors had been sheared away, then covered with a glass dome.

Pale sunlight sparkled off the dome. It was almost like a beacon.

Humans and Hork-Bajir walked the street, side by side. But not in large numbers. In fact, the entire city seemed far emptier than it should have been.

We turned a corner and froze.

"That's where the City Arena should be," I said. "It's where we saw the circus."

"The Arena. That big department store. That building that used to have the tall antennas on top. They're all gone," Marco said. "Just . . . gone."

In their place was a Yeerk pool.

A pool of shocking size. It was a small lake, really. You could have ridden around on it in a motorboat and not looked out of place.

It was three times as wide as a football field is long. Maybe four times as wide. And all around it were cages, just like the underground Yeerk pool we knew too well.

But there was a difference here. The humans and Hork-Bajir in these cages no longer called for help. They cried, they sobbed, or more often they just stared blankly into space. But they did not call for help.

They knew there was no help coming. They knew that hope was dead.

We just stared, the six of us. Just stared emptily.

A Human-Controller brushed past us, jostling me as she went.

"Excuse *me*," I said in a sarcastic voice. A mistake. I knew it was a mistake as soon as the two little words were out of my mouth.

The woman stopped. She came back toward us.

"What did you say?" she demanded.

"Nothing," I said.

But she kept staring at me through narrowed eyes. "What is your name?"

I knew that answering "Rachel" was not going to work. She wanted my Yeerk name. I tensed up, ready for a fight.

"Her name is not your concern," Tobias said.

The woman sneered. "Oh? And why is that? You are spies, that's what you are. Spies!"

"Her name is not your concern," Tobias repeated. "*His* name is your concern." He jerked his thumb at Ax. "Because his name . . . is Visser Three."

CHAPTER 20

"Visser Three?" the woman repeated skeptically.

It took me a few seconds to track. What was Tobias talking about? Why was he saying Ax was Visser Three?

Fortunately, Ax caught on more quickly. He immediately began to demorph and return to Andalite form. And as soon as the Andalite stalk eyes appeared, the woman began to tremble.

"But . . . but . . . you said Visser *Three*. Only Visser *One* has an Andalite host body!"

Great. Visser Three had been promoted.

"Yeah," I said to the woman. "But he was Visser

Three back in the old days. Back when we were all friends. Comrades in arms."

"I . . . we . . . no one told us you were visiting Earth, Visser," the woman babbled.

She was clearly terrified. Obviously Visser Three's reputation had not softened any over the years.

Ax had regained his full Andalite form. And the various Controllers on the street were staring in a mixture of fascination and fear.

"If I had known . . ." the woman moaned. "I would never . . ."

Ax waved his hand dismissively. <Silence. You are right to remain vigilant. If you had not been vigilant I would have destroyed you for being a careless fool. Now get out of here.>

"Yes, my Visser! Yes!" The woman took off. Fast.

Which left us standing around in the street, gaping at the Yeerk pool. And a lot of Controllers gaping at us.

"This isn't good," Marco said. "Word is going to travel very fast that Visser Three is here. And someone is going to realize the truth."

"So what *now*?" Jake wondered. "How long does the Ellimist want to leave us here?"

"Until we are convinced he's right," Tobias said.

"There must be something more he wants us to see," Cassie said.

I glanced at Cassie. She looked puzzled. I guess I expected her to look like, "See, I told you so, here's the future." But she seemed troubled. Like she couldn't make sense of something that was bothering her.

"What?" I asked her.

She shrugged. "Just a feeling. There's something deeper going on here. Something we don't get."

The Yeerk pool was a busy little place. Controllers coming and going. The host bodies were shoved into cages, and dragged back out when it was time. There was a steady procession along the six different piers, draining out and taking in Yeerks.

Over it all loomed the EGS Tower, topped off by the glass dome.

"Why put a Yeerk pool here?" I wondered aloud. "I mean, there's all kinds of open areas. Why go to the trouble of removing the buildings that were here? It's not like this is exactly a scenic location."

"I wonder what year it is?" Marco said. "Is this next year? Ten years from now? Twenty?"

I heard a low roar coming from the sky. A Yeerk Bug fighter swooped down low, took a turn around the EGS Tower, and settled toward the near side of the Yeerk pool.

I don't know why, but I felt drawn to that Bug fighter. Maybe it was some strange psychic urging.

Maybe it was the Ellimist, making me go closer to see what he wanted to show me.

Wherever the urge came from, I found myself walking toward the Bug fighter.

"Hey!" Jake said. "What are you doing?"

"You guys stay back," I said.

"It's okay," Marco said, jerking his thumb at Ax. "We're with Visser Three here. Excuse me, I mean Visser One. And congrats on the big promotion, by the way."

Ax stepped out quickly in front of me, swaggering and acting the role of the great and terrible Visser.

As we drew closer to the pool, there was a crowd of Controllers, humans, Hork-Bajir, Taxxons, and a few odd species I had never seen. The crowd parted very quickly. No one wanted to accidentally annoy Visser One in any way.

We swaggered up to the Bug fighter like the bosses of all the world. Then the door of the Bug fighter opened.

I stopped. Ax stopped as well. The others crowded behind us.

My skin was tingling. My hair felt like it was standing on end. I knew something was about to happen. Something awesome and horrible.

And then, they stepped from the Bug fighter. A human and an Andalite. I knew the Andalite. We had met before. I could feel the dark dread that emanated from him.

Visser Three. The *real* Visser Three.

Seeing Ax along with Visser Three, the crowd of Controllers immediately knew the difference. Visser Three has an Andalite body, but there is no mistaking him for anything other than a creature of pure evil.

<Well, well,> Visser Three said to the person with him. <Right on schedule. Just as you said it would be.>

I stared at the human. She was a pretty young woman, maybe twenty or twenty-two years old. She had blond hair, cut short. She wore no makeup. Her clothes were plain.

I had stopped breathing. My heart had stopped beating. I tried to swallow but couldn't.

"Hello, Rachel," the woman said to me.

"Hello, Rachel," I replied.

CHAPTER 21

It was me. Me, as I would be in the future.

"I knew you were coming," the future Rachel said. "After all, I *was* you. Once I stood right where you stand now, and looked just like you look now, and saw myself as I am today."

She sounded perfectly calm. But her eyes flickered quickly to Ax, then back to me.

Visser Three shook his head in amusement. <If only I had known from the start that you were humans. For so long I believed you were Andalites. Until, at last, we caught you.>

I felt strangely calm. I mean, considering what

was happening. I was face-to-face with Visser Three—who was now Visser One. I was face-to-face with my own future.

"You're a Controller," I said to the older me.

"Of course," she said. She smiled. A cruel smile, not at all like me. "We won. You all led us on a nice chase, but in the end, we won. This planet is Yeerk territory. The human race has achieved its destiny as hosts for the Yeerk race."

"If you know so much, how did we come to be here? In the future?" Marco asked.

<An Ellimist has brought you here,> Visser Three said. <In your own time, you face a choice. The Ellimist has brought you six humans . . . you five humans and one Andalite . . . here to show you a future. To show you *the* future. Soon he will return you to your own time.>

"What choice did we make?" I asked.

The older Rachel smiled her cruel smile. "The right one, obviously. Everything has worked out perfectly."

"Yeah?" Jake said defiantly. "Maybe not. The Ellimist brought us here to help us make a choice. So what if we go back to our own time and decide to accept the Ellimist's offer? Then Rachel won't be around to be turned into a Controller. She'll be with the rest of us on whatever planet the Ellimist takes us to."

I watched closely for any reaction by my older self. Nothing. Not a flicker. And yet, there was something. She was trying to hide something.

"You know what we decided. But still, here you are," I said. "So either you're here to change what I decided. Except . . . no, then it might change all of this. Or else you're here because your being here is what caused me to decide whatever I decided."

<Confusing, isn't it?> Visser Three sneered. <I don't know how the Ellimists keep it all straight.>

"Let's leave," Cassie said suddenly. "I don't like this place, and I don't like these two . . . creatures."

"But, Cassie, I'm your best friend," my older self said mockingly.

"No, you're not. Maybe Rachel is still alive in there somewhere. But what you are is a Yeerk."

Cassie started to turn away. As she did, she tripped. She fell against me. Suddenly the older Rachel was there. She grabbed me and held my arm steady so I didn't fall.

But to Ax it must have looked like she was lunging at me. His tail whipped forward in the blink of an eye.

Ax's quivering blade was pressed against the older Rachel's throat.

Her eyes went wide with fear. She shot a glance at Visser Three. And to my amazement, Visser Three seemed frozen. He was confused. His main eyes narrowed. He looked from Ax, to the older Rachel, to me.

Suddenly I knew. "This wasn't in the script, was it?" I asked him. "This wasn't supposed to happen. Something has changed! It's Ax, isn't it? You said 'six humans' before. That's what you expected to find. That's what Rachel told you would happen. But the future has changed, hasn't it? Something is different."

Visser Three glared at me, and now he dropped the pretense of politeness. <Do you know what I did when I finally caught you and your little band of Animorphs? Do you know what I did? I gave each of you to a trusted lieutenant. And once you belonged to us, once you were MINE, I killed your bird friend here and we roasted his body.>

Visser Three leaned close to me. <He was tough and stringy, but we added a sauce you humans have. Barbecue, I believe it's called. And then your friend Tobias was delicious. You had a leg, as I recall. You ate it and laughed.>

I really wanted to morph right then. I really wanted to become the grizzly and tear Visser Three a few new holes. But there were hundreds of Controllers around. And while I was morphing I would be vulnerable.

Ax still had his tail blade pressed against the older Rachel's throat. <He can't hurt us,> Ax said. <He can't do a thing to us. If he does, he would change

history. He doesn't know how that would work out.>

"Good point, Ax," Jake said. He met my gaze. He had a dangerous, angry look in his eyes. "He can't hurt us. But the reverse . . . well . . ."

"Excellent point," I agreed. I focused my mind on the grizzly bear. "So, Visser Three. You killed my friend Tobias and roasted him over a fire."

I was beginning to change. So was Jake.

<I have a hundred Hork-Bajir I can call!> Visser Three said.

"So call them," Marco said. "Maybe one of them will get careless with a Dracon beam and kill one of us. How do you suppose that will change the past? Hard to tell, isn't it?"

Claws had sprouted from my fingers. Coarse brown fur was covering my body. I could feel the surge of power as I became more bear than human.

"Visser," the older Rachel said tersely. "What do we do?"

<We?> Visser Three said. <We do nothing. I retreat.>

Visser Three began backing away. But I wasn't about to let him go. I had him. After all the pain he had caused, I had him. After all the damage he had done, he was now powerless.

I did not wait until the last of my human features was submerged. I was bear enough. I charged.

Bears are very large and look sort of clumsy. But they can be very fast.

<Now, you filth, let's see who eats who.>

I barreled toward him. He turned to run. But he had turned too late.

I hit him. Eight hundred pounds of fast-moving bear hit Visser Three in the flank and brought him down hard.

I drew back one huge claw and swung with all my might.

My hand slapped the trunk of a tree. My human hand.

"Owww!"

I was human again. I was in the woods behind Cassie's farm. The others were all there as well. Tobias, once again a hawk, perched in a branch overhead.

"No! I'm sick of this!" I yelled. I slammed the tree again in sheer frustration. "I'm sick of this! I *had* him!"

Cassie came over and put her arm around my shoulders. "It doesn't matter. That's a Visser Three who doesn't exist yet."

"I'm so sick of this," I said again, a little more softly. "What's the point? What's the point in anything? We know the future now. We know what happens if we decide to stay and fight."

I felt lost. The last ounce of energy just seeped

away from me. It was too much. Too many things to deal with. And what was the point? What did it even matter what I did?

I flopped down onto the grass and pine needle–covered ground, and rested my head in my hands. I was done. Done trying to make sense of a world where I could be jerked back and forth like a puppet.

The six of us just lay there on the floor of pine needles for a while. Staring. Thinking. Letting it all sink in.

It was over.

The war was done. And we had lost.

<It could all still be an Ellimist trick,> Ax said halfheartedly.

"No," I said flatly. "You know it's not a trick, Ax. At least not the way you mean. If the Ellimist wanted to force us to do something, he has more than enough power."

"We need to think this through," Jake said wearily.

I shrugged. "You think it through. I'm tired of thinking. I was just about to vote when the Ellimist dragged us off for his little show-and-tell. I was about to be good old Rachel and vote no. I was going to be tough, one more time. But I'm changing my vote. I'm not going to end up as a Controller. That's not going to happen. Not to me. If that means I'm running away, too bad. I change my vote."

You know what? At that moment of surrender, I felt good. I wish I could say I didn't. But I felt a wave of relief wash over me. No more hard decisions. No more danger. No more having to be brave.

"That makes it Cassie, Rachel, and me, in favor," Marco said. "Three to two, unless Ax is voting."

<I follow Prince Jake,> Ax said.

<Maybe . . .> Tobias began. <Maybe if some of the human race survives on some other planet . . . Maybe it will be like when they brought wolves back to live in national parks. I mean, maybe someday we can return and take Earth back.>

"Are you changing your vote, Tobias?" Jake asked him.

<Jake, you know I would never run from a fight. . . .>

We all just sat there, staring at nothing. We were going to do it. We were going to abandon the fight. We all knew it.

Jake hung his head. "Ellimist?" he said softly to the air, "We have decided. The answer is yes."

The Ellimist had said we would be transported immediately, once we decided. I expected my next breath to be drawn on some distant planet.

But nothing happened.

Nothing at all.

CHAPTER 22

I can't tell you how weird it was, going to school the next day. Sitting in class, trying to pay attention while my teacher, Ms. Paloma, talked about what led up to the Second World War.

"Maybe if the United States had been ready to fight earlier," she said, "the war would have ended earlier and fewer people would have been killed. But our country wanted peace."

I just kept looking at her and wondering, *Was that your skeleton draped across the desk?*

What was the point of going to school? What was the point in anything? I had seen the future. I knew how it all turned out. The human race was done for.

Finished. That was where all our long history led — to a Yeerk pool.

"Because we were so devoted to peace, we may have actually made the war worse," Ms. Paloma droned on. "We'll never know for sure, of course. You can't really second-guess history."

You can if you're an Ellimist, I thought. *If you're an Ellimist, you can look ahead and see it all.*

"Why not?"

It was Cassie's voice. I glanced across the room at her. She had that same look of confusion I'd seen the day before. The frustrated look, like she sensed something she couldn't quite grasp yet.

"Why can't you second-guess history? I mean, if you *could* go back and change things so that the U.S. was ready to fight earlier . . ."

Ms. Paloma sat on the edge of her desk. "Because events are intertwined in ways we cannot always see, Cassie. Sometimes small things can make huge differences. You know, they say that a single butterfly, beating its wings in China, may affect the way the wind blows here in our country. A single butterfly beating its wings may make a tiny change that becomes a bigger change that becomes a tornado. The world isn't like arithmetic. It isn't just one plus one equals two. It's more complicated than that."

And then the oddest thing happened. Ms. Paloma looked right at me. Right into my eyes.

"Much more complicated than that," she said. "A single butterfly . . . a single butterfly . . . a single butterfly . . ."

The hair on the back of my neck was tingling. Everyone was looking at her like she was crazy.

Suddenly Ms. Paloma shook her head, like she was popping out of a trance. She smiled a confused smile. "Okay, well, anyway, you all have the reading assignments."

The bell rang and I practically jerked up out of my seat.

Cassie threaded her way through the kids who were rushing out of the room.

"Okay, tell me *that* wasn't weird," Cassie whispered.

"I thought maybe I was imagining it," I said. "Besides, who knows what's weird anymore? I'm sitting there waiting for the . . . you know who . . . to suddenly zap us out of here."

Cassie nodded. "So why hasn't he?"

Out in the fast-moving crush of bodies in the hall, we made our way to our lockers.

"I don't know," I said as I spun my combination lock. "We decided to say yes. We're giving him what he wants."

I popped my locker door open.

"Unless . . ." Cassie said.

"Unless maybe that wasn't the answer he wanted," I finished her thought.

"But it's nuts," Cassie said, frowning. "Everything he did made it look like he wanted us to say yes. He appears the first time right as we're about to be swallowed by a . . ." She looked around to make sure no one could overhear. "Just as we were about to be swallowed. I mean, come on. Obviously he must have figured we'd want to bail."

"We might have," I said. "Except we saw that dropshaft. So we thought we could escape. Otherwise . . ." I stopped talking. I stared at Cassie. She stared back.

"He *showed* us the dropshaft!" Cassie said.

"Why?" I wondered aloud. "Why? What is he doing with us? He appears when we're desperate. He says he doesn't interfere and gives us a choice. Then he lets us see a way out. What's that all about?"

"Then he gives us another chance. He shows us the future. He shows us . . . you, basically. You in the future. So we *know* for sure that we must have decided to stay and fight. And we *know* we lost. And all of that means we have to say yes and let him take us away. So why have I been feeling like I was missing something?"

The warning bell for next period rang.

"This is insane, as Marco would say."

Cassie laughed. "Yeah. I have gym next period. At any moment I might suddenly be swooped away to another planet, but in the meantime I have to go play volleyball."

I watched her walk away. Then I hurried to my next class.

A single butterfly, I thought.

But how is the butterfly supposed to know when to beat her wings?

CHAPTER 23

I was back in the underground Yeerk pool. Trapped. Stuck to the Taxxon's tongue. But not a cockroach. I was myself, in my human body, only tiny. Stuck. About to die.

Ax was talking. <Yeerk pool. It's the center of their lives. Almost a religion.>

I squirmed and tried to get away. I tried to change into something else. The bear. I wanted to become the bear. But I was stuck. All I could do was beat my helpless butterfly wings.

He showed us the dropshaft, Cassie's voice murmured in the back of my head.

I swirled down dark corridors. I flew wildly on

138

butterfly wings, always chasing a light that never drew closer and yet never disappeared.

The Kandrona, I thought in my dream. *The light is the Kandrona.*

"The center of their lives. Almost a religion."

<No, not the Yeerk pool, really. The Kandrona. That is the center for them. That is their light.>

"He showed us the dropshaft," Cassie said again, only now she was Ms. Paloma.

My eyes snapped open.

I sat up in my bed.

I was as awake as I'd ever been. I was electric!

"Hah HAH!" I yelled in the darkness of my room. "YES!"

Then I hesitated. Was I nuts? Was I just desperate? I ran through it all again.

"Got 'em!" I whispered. "Oh, man, we got 'em! Got the disgusting worms!"

I shucked off the T-shirt that I wear to bed, and quickly slipped into my morphing outfit.

I threw open the window. Then I paused. It would be Saturday morning in a few hours. No school. But if my mom found me gone, she might worry.

I quickly scribbled a note saying I had gone for an early-morning run. That I might go over to Cassie's afterward.

And then I glanced at the picture on my desk. The

one of three-year-old me on the balance beam, being held up by my proud father.

I could *not* tell the others. We had already decided. We were going to say yes to the Ellimist. We would let him take us to a place where there would be no battles and no need to decide.

If I told my friends what I suspected . . .

I felt the weight come down on me again. The weight of uncertainty and guilt and fear.

I looked at the picture of my dad and smiled. "What would you think of me, Dad, if I walked away, when I still had a chance to win?"

And then I morphed. My arms shrank. My skin began to flow into patterns of soft feathers that could ride silently on the night breeze.

In a few more minutes, I was ready.

The moon was bright in the sky. Dawn was still hours away. A perfect night for an owl. But I paid no attention to the juicy prey below me as I flew at top speed toward the woods.

<Tobias! It's me! Don't panic, but wake up!>

<What the . . . ! Didn't I tell you about zooming up in—>

<Come on!> I yelled.

<Come on, where?>

<Don't argue, just come on. I know you don't like to fly at night, but just come on, anyway!>

<Rachel, have you lost your mind? Where are we going?>

<We're going to be butterflies, Tobias. We're going to Cassie's barn, and then we're going to change history.>

He opened his wings and flew alongside me, just a few feet away.

<Whatever you say, Rachel,> Tobias said grumpily. <But what makes you think —>

<I know where it is, Tobias,> I interrupted him.

<Where *what* is?>

<Tobias? I know the location of the Kandrona.>

CHAPTER 24

$\bigcup$kay, it's three forty-seven in the morning," Marco said. "And I'm here, thanks to the fact that my dad is a sound sleeper who doesn't notice when I wake up screaming because an owl and a hawk have just flown through my window. So now maybe you can tell us all *why* we're here?"

Everyone was there in Cassie's barn. Jake looked sleepy but interested. Cassie was using the time to check on some of the sick animals. Ax just stood to one side, waiting to see what Jake told him to do. Tobias perched on an overhead beam, tired from having flown too much.

We were lit by a single small bulb that never even

touched the shadows in the corners of the barn. We didn't want to take the chance that Cassie's parents might notice a light on and come to investigate.

"Yes," I answered Marco, "I'll tell you why you're here. I know where the Kandrona is. I *know* where it is."

That got his attention. But he was still skeptical. "What makes you think you know where the Kandrona is?"

"The Ellimist. He showed us. We all thought it was unfair when he appeared in the Yeerk pool and asked us to decide when we were about to be eaten, right?"

<I told you, Ellimists care nothing about fairness,> Ax said.

"No. You're wrong, Ax. At least this time. The Ellimist appeared when we were about to be swallowed by the Taxxon. But then he showed us the dropshaft."

"We saw the dropshaft because it was there," Jake argued. "It wasn't about him showing it to us."

"Are you sure?" I asked. "He waited till we had walked out of the Yeerk lunchroom to appear. He waited till we were standing where we were sure to notice the dropshaft."

I saw Jake raise an eyebrow thoughtfully. He and Marco exchanged a look.

"What if we're wrong about the Ellimist being unfair? What if Cassie's instinct is right — that he is telling the truth? That he's trying to do what's right? He tells us that in the future we lose the fight. That the human race is enslaved. That he has a way to save a small number of us by taking us to a safe place. And it's all true."

"If he's telling us the truth, that we lose in the future, what's this all about?" Marco asked. "We've seen that future. Nothing we do will matter."

I shook my head. "No. It will matter. If it didn't matter how we decided, why even bother to ask us what we wanted to do? See? It does matter what we do."

"Yes," Marco said. "But the answer is obvious. We can only change the future by agreeing to the Ellimist's plan to take us to a safe planet."

"Yes, that's one way. He offered us that. But when we finally accepted, he didn't act. He didn't take us instantly away. Why? Why, after we agreed, did he leave us here?"

"Because he wanted a different answer," Cassie said, nodding at me and giving me a wink. "That's what's been eating at me."

"What different answer?" Marco asked.

"He's in a trap," Cassie said. "The Ellimist is trapped. He *wants* to save Earth. But he can't interfere directly. Supposedly all he's allowed to do is offer to save a small number of us. But he knows that won't save Earth. It will save a few humans, yes, but when he showed us visions of Earth, he wasn't talking just about humans. He said Earth was a work of art. He wants to find a way to save it."

"Without interfering directly," I agreed. "But what if we just happened to see another way? What if the Ellimist showed us the future, trying to convince us to let him take us away, and we just *happened* to see a way out?"

"What way out?" Jake demanded.

"The Kandrona. He let us see where the Kandrona is," I said. "That Yeerk pool downtown, that's the key. Why build a Yeerk pool downtown? Why level so many buildings to make room for it? Why leave the EGS Tower still standing? And why is there a glass dome on the top floors of the EGS? Ax is the one who said it — the Yeerk pool is the center of their lives. That Yeerk pool? I think it's a shrine. Almost a holy place to them. It's where they located the first Kandrona to be placed on planet Earth."

Jake snapped his fingers. "The EGS Tower!"

"*That's* what's under that dome on the top floors. The Kandrona. *That's* what the Ellimist wanted us to see. Just the way he let us see the dropshaft we used to escape. He wasn't interfering . . . technically. The choice is still ours."

Marco laughed out loud. "You mean maybe the Ellimist is bending his own rules? So he can say, 'Hey, I didn't interfere,' but at the same time he's putting us where we can figure it out? I can't believe it! The Ellimist is a weasel! He found a loophole! I think I like that guy."

"But even if you're right about the Kandrona, Rachel," Jake argued, "what does it prove? If we destroy it, are we sure it will change the future?"

Cassie looked at me and smiled. "Maybe yes, maybe no," she said. "But things are connected in millions of ways. They say a single butterfly, beating its wings in China, can start a tornado in America."

<Yes,> Tobias said, <but how does the butterfly know when to beat its wings?>

"It doesn't," I said. "I guess it beats its wings the best it can, and hopes it will all work out. It's a butterfly. It just does what butterflies do."

"And what do *we* do, Xena, Warrior Princess?" Marco asked mockingly, knowing the answer I would give.

"We kick Yeerk butt," I said with a grin.

CHAPTER 25

At 5:10 in the morning, the EGS Tower's windows were almost all dark. From the deeply shadowed plaza in front of the building, we could see a sleepy, uniformed guard inside the lobby.

"There are dozens of businesses and law firms and stuff in this building," Jake warned. "Most of them are probably just normal people. Fortunately, at this time of day, almost no one will be here. But the guard is probably just a normal guy."

"How do we deal with him without hurting him?" Cassie asked.

Suddenly Tobias swooped down out of a dark sky. <I can't see anything useful through the windows up

there,> he said. <Too bad that glass dome is still in the future. But I can tell you one thing. Something up there is giving off some heat. I'm getting a beautiful updraft from the building itself.>

"Let's do this, already," I grumbled. I started morphing into the bear.

"Okay, but take it easy on any innocent bystanders," Jake said. "Tobias? I know you're wearing out, but stay up and keep an eye out while we morph."

<No prob, Jake.> He flapped his wings and slowly gained altitude.

"These doors will be locked," Cassie pointed out.

"Not for long," I said.

Ax was already demorphing, coming out of his human body and resuming his Andalite shape.

Jake's eyes were glittering, his body was lengthening, and striped orange and black fur was spreading like a wave over his skin.

Cassie was already on all fours. Rough gray fur grew thickly around her shoulders. Her mouth bulged out farther and farther to form a wolf's muzzle.

<Hey! A guy's coming up behind you,> Tobias called down. <I think he's drunk. He's carrying a bottle. If it were daytime, I could read the label. He's definitely staggering.>

<Keep morphing,> Jake said quickly. <Cassie? See if you can get rid of him.>

Cassie trotted off, already fully morphed. And a second later we heard, "Grrrrrr, grrrrrr, grrrOWW-WRR!" followed by "Whoa! No way!" and the sound of a crashing bottle and running feet.

Cassie returned just as we were finishing our morphs. <He decided to go in a different direction,> Cassie reported.

<Okay, so let's go in,> I said. I was fully the grizzly now, and feeling invulnerable.

<Actually, how about if Marco tries it first?> Jake suggested.

While the rest of us lurked in the shadows, Marco, now an extremely large, powerful gorilla, knuckle-walked to the glass door. He stood up on his hind legs and tapped with one massive finger on the glass.

The guard jerked in his seat. He stood up and moved cautiously closer. Then he drew his gun.

"Hey, get out of here," the guard said.

<Hi,> Marco said in thought-speak. <I just came from a masquerade party, and I was looking for Visser Three.>

The guard's eyes went wide. "Andalite!" he hissed.

<Oh, so you *are* a Controller. Good. That makes it so much simpler.>

With that, Marco punched straight through the thick glass of the door.

CRASH!

His gorilla fist connected squarely with the guard's chin. The guard crumpled, still holding his gun.

<Move, move, move!> Jake yelled.

I barreled into the rest of the glass door. I was careful, but not too careful. I wasn't very worried about being hurt. Shattered glass flew everywhere.

Cassie, Ax, and Jake leaped over the glass shards. Jake raced for the elevator.

<There may be an alarm. We have to move fast,> Jake said.

<We'll never fit in one elevator,> Marco said.

<Head for the freight elevator. That'll hold us,> Jake said. <Go for the top floor.>

Cassie and Ax kept an eye on all activity on the ground floor while they waited for the elevator to come back down. Jake, Marco, and I had the most firepower — so we went in first.

We squeezed our combined bulk into the one freight elevator car — not an easy thing to do — but we managed it.

<Can you press the button? I sure can't,> Jake said. He held up one of his huge paws to show me.

It wasn't easy. Bear paws aren't exactly subtle tools. But after carefully lining up my first claw, I hit the top button.

The doors closed and we rose swiftly upward.

There was a safety inspection certificate mounted on one wall. I leaned very close to make out the letters, and read it aloud. <Says here the maximum load is twenty people.>

<How many bears, tigers, and gorillas?>

The ride seemed to be taking forever. I watched the counter tick off the floors. Twenty-one. Twenty-two. Twenty-three.

<So. Seen any good movies lately?> Jake asked.

<I want to go see that new Keanu Reeves movie,> I said.

<He's supposed to be cute, right?>

<Duh,> I said. <I wonder if he'd ever want to go out with a girl like me. You know, lots of guys wouldn't want to date a grizzly bear.>

Suddenly I realized there was music playing in the elevator. The usual stupid elevator music.

<Get ready,> Jake said.

<Been ready.>

<Top floor. Ladies' shoes. Children's apparel. Everyone out,> Marco announced in his best elevator operator's voice.

The elevator stopped. The door opened.

Just as three humans and two Hork-Bajir were racing toward the elevator.

"Rrrrrrooooowwwwrrrr!" Jake roared in a voice that could crack concrete.

"Rrrrrooooowwwwrrr!" I echoed in my own muddier bear voice.

I charged like an enraged bull. I went straight for the nearest Hork-Bajir. That meant running *through* the closest human. I felt a slight thump as his body was knocked aside.

I slammed into the Hork-Bajir. The force of my charge just picked him up and carried him along till I hammered into the far wall.

It didn't kill him, but he wasn't going anywhere.

Jake took down the other Hork-Bajir with a lightning swipe of his claws. The remaining humans bolted.

<I'm cut,> Jake said.

<Is it bad?>

<It isn't good,> Jake said. <But I'll be okay for a while.>

Just then the elevator door opened and Ax and Cassie piled out.

<About time,> I said. <We've taken care of the welcoming committee.>

<Sorry. Ax pushed the button for the wrong floor,> Cassie said. She glanced at the two Hork-Bajir. <You *know* they have more than those two up here guarding the Kandrona and . . . Jake! You're bleeding,> Cassie cried.

<I'm fine. The Human-Controllers ran down that

hallway,> Jake said. <Let's go. We haven't won this battle yet.>

I took off at a loping run. The others were right behind me. My claws gouged the carpeted floor with every step. I couldn't see well, but I could smell the adrenaline of the frightened Human-Controllers. I knew where they had gone.

I could smell them. I could sense them. They had challenged me. And I was going to show them who was boss.

<Watch out, Rachel,> Cassie called. <There's a door straight ahead of you.>

<Nah. There's no door,> I said, and plowed all my eight hundred pounds into a steel door that popped open like the lid of a jack-in-the-box.

Inside, eight Hork-Bajir warriors stood ready.

Eight walking razor blades.

Eight of them. Five of us. No way we could win. A sensible person would have seen the odds and run away. But I charged straight at them.

Later, everyone thought I was being brave. But you know what the truth was? The truth was, with my weak bear eyesight, all I could see was a blur. I thought they were humans.

I wasn't brave. I was just blind.

CHAPTER 26

Rachel!> Cassie yelled a warning.

<Too late to retreat,> Jake said. <GO!>

I figured out the eight blurry figures were Hork-Bajir when I was about three feet away from slamming into the first one. By then it was too late to stop.

"Kill the *gaffnur* Andalites!" a Hork-Bajir cried in the weird mix of languages that they use. "Kill *fraghent* Andalite *halaf* kill all!"

Suddenly I realized I was cut. A searing pain radiated from my shoulder.

I swung my paw and hit the Hork-Bajir in the head. He fell, but as he fell he slashed with his tyrannosaurus feet, and ripped a second cut in me.

<Aaarrrgghhh!>

From that point on, it was a nightmare of terrible images that seemed to float in and out of my hazy vision.

I saw Cassie, with her bone-breaking jaws sunk into the throat of a Hork-Bajir.

I saw Ax, his tail like a deadly bullwhip, lashing, cutting, lashing again, till one of the Hork-Bajir stood screaming, holding his own severed arm.

I saw Jake and a Hork-Bajir locked in a deadly embrace as they rolled and slashed at each other with superhuman speed.

I saw Marco fighting with one arm as he held his own sliced stomach together with the other hand.

And everywhere, snarling, growling, raging, roaring noise.

<Look out! Rachel, behind you!>

"Die, *gaferach*, die!"

"RRRROOOWWRRR!"

<Help! He's on me!>

<Aaaahhhhhh!>

I couldn't tell who was winning. I couldn't tell who was hurt. It all became one long cry, one long scream of rage. Hork-Bajir and Animorph. Alien and animal.

We were flesh-and-blood creatures thrown into

a meat grinder. Thirteen deadly animals locked in a combat to the death.

I felt the bear weakening as he was cut again and again by Hork-Bajir blades. I was losing blood. The human part of me knew that. I could feel my strength ebbing.

I charged again and hit a Hork-Bajir in the stomach. I carried him along with my momentum as he slashed wildly at me.

CRAAAASSSSHHHH!

I'd hit something! Glass. It had shattered.

A window! I had shoved the Hork-Bajir through the window.

"AAAAAAaaaarrrrr!"

I heard the Hork-Bajir's cry, dying away as it fell.

A sudden flash of movement, as something came zooming through the shattered window.

"Tseeeeeerrr!" Tobias screamed as he spread his talons forward and struck the closest Hork-Bajir, raking his eyes.

The battle had turned!

The Hork-Bajir had had enough. Maybe it was hearing one of their fellows fall sixty stories. Or maybe it was Tobias's arrival, strengthening our side. But whatever it was, the remaining Hork-Bajir ran.

Three of them ran. The rest would not be running anywhere.

Marco grabbed the crumpled door and slammed it back in place. Then, with what must have been the last of his strength, he shoved a desk in place to block the door.

<I'm hurt bad,> Marco said. <I gotta morph out, man.>

<Do it,> Jake said. <Everyone. Demorph.>

<I'm okay,> I said weakly.

<Rachel,> Tobias said. <Your left arm.>

I stared blankly at my left paw. It wasn't there. It was a stump.

<Demorphing,> I said. I focused on my human body. My weak but healthy human body.

Morphing is done from DNA, fortunately. DNA is not affected by injuries, so injuries do not follow you from one morph to another.

Exhaustion does.

As my human body emerged from the vast bulk of the grizzly, I felt so weary I was afraid I might faint.

Through human eyes, I saw a scene of carnage. The Hork-Bajir lay sprawled around the room. Most seemed to be breathing. None were conscious. All were bleeding from claw-and-teeth wounds.

Unfortunately for the Hork-Bajir, they could not simply morph out of their injured bodies.

"Everyone okay?" Jake asked, sounding as weary as I felt.

"Yeah, but that was way too close," Cassie said.

We were in a large office. I could see that now with my human eyes. Desks lay splintered. The carpet was ripped into ribbons. The walls were gouged.

Floor-to-ceiling windows formed one wall. They were shattered. I remembered the Hork-Bajir falling, and shuddered.

There was a door in one wall.

"Through there?" Marco suggested.

"Let's try it," I said. I staggered toward the door. It was not locked.

A bare room. Tile floor. White painted walls. The wall of windows was blocked by heavy curtains. The room was empty but for a large, massively built platform in the very center.

It was a steel pedestal, maybe three feet high, eight feet long.

And atop that pedestal was a machine the size of a small car. It was shaped like a cylinder, tapered to dull points on both ends.

It gleamed brightly, like new chrome, as if it had just been polished. And it made a slight, low humming noise. As I approached I felt my hair stand on end from the static electricity. It was warm in the room, very warm. It smelled like lightning.

<The Kandrona,> Ax said.

"The Kandrona," I echoed.

For a full minute we all just stood there, gaping at it.

"Rachel?" Jake said at last. "We need you to morph again. Can you do it?"

I nodded slowly. "Elephant?"

"Elephant. I don't know how else we're going to do it. We don't have any tools or anything."

I morphed the elephant.

Tobias flew outside to make sure there were no pedestrians below on the dark sidewalk.

It took every last ounce of power that elephant had. But the Kandrona did move.

It did, slowly, in jerks and starts, slide across the floor.

And when at last I shoved it through the windows, it did fall the sixty stories, to smash into the concrete below.

CHAPTER 27

"We did it," I whispered as I returned to my normal body. "We destroyed the Kandrona."

"We have to get out of here," Jake said. "The Yeerks will know. They'll be all over this place."

"So, what does this mean?" Marco asked. "We did it. But, what does it mean? Have we changed the future?"

EVERYTHING CHANGES THE FUTURE.

I groaned. "Somehow I knew we'd hear from that guy again."

A REPLACEMENT KANDRONA WILL BE HERE IN THREE OF YOUR WEEKS. IT WAS ALREADY ON ITS WAY.

"Are you telling us this was all a waste?" Marco demanded.

Ax said, <No, Marco, it was not a waste. Three weeks with only the Kandrona aboard the mother ship? In three weeks' time they will suffer greatly. They will fall behind in their schedule. Many Yeerks will perish. Three weeks is not a waste.>

"Don't you mean three of *our* weeks, Ax?" Marco teased.

"Is it enough?" Jake demanded loudly. "Is it enough? Have we changed the future?"

There was no answer. Just silence.

"I don't think he knows," I said. "He showed us a possible future. But you know what? I don't believe the Ellimist really knows the future any more than we do."

"What makes you so sure?"

I laughed. "Because wherever it is that the Ellimist exists, and whatever he's up to, and whatever game he's playing, and no matter how mighty he is, he has butterflies, too."

Then, an amazing thing. Laughter that welled up from inside us, and echoed through us, and made us all smile as if we were fresh and full of energy.

HA, HA, HA, HA. AS I SAID, YOU ARE A PRIMITIVE RACE, AND YET YOU ARE CAPABLE OF LEARNING.

I smiled. "Come on, guys. Do you have the energy for one more morph? I feel like flying."

At first we saw no evidence that the Yeerks were suffering. I don't know how they did it, but the Yeerks managed to maintain. It wasn't until later that we learned we had done them terrible damage.

But that is another story.

Two days later, I took the bus over to my dad's apartment. He was packing up his suitcase to leave.

"Hi, Rachel," he said when he opened his door. "I wasn't sure you were coming over."

I shrugged. "You're too disorganized to be able to pack all by yourself."

He smiled a sad smile. "Thanks."

"Yeah. No big thing."

"I would have come and picked you up," he said. "Sweetheart," my dad said, "you know you can always change your mind. You can always come live with me."

"I know, Dad."

He smiled sadly. "You know I'll miss seeing you as much. Even though I'll be here every chance I get."

"I know that, too, Dad," I said. I gave him a little kiss on his cheek. He patted my hair and I cried.

I closed up his suitcase and zipped it.

"You going to be okay without me here to take care of you?" he asked.

"I can take care of myself," I said, wiping away the tears.

We took the elevator down to a taxi that was waiting.

"Come with me to the airport. I'll send you home in the cab."

I shook my head. "No, I have stuff to do."

He smiled. "I understand. You probably have something very important to do with your friends." It was a joke.

"Absolutely," I said. "We have to save the world."

My dad laughed. "If anyone can do it, honey, it would be you."

Then the taxi drove off.

I looked up in the sky. A lone hawk circled high overhead.

<You coming, Rachel?> Tobias called down to me in thought-speak.

I nodded my head so he could see. Yes. I was coming.

<LEARN THE TRUTH.>
Don't miss

ANIMORPHS™ #08

THE
ALIEN

*B*efore Earth . . .

<Prepare for return to normal space,> Captain Nerefir said in thought-speak.

I was on the bridge of our Dome ship. It was an amazing moment. I had never been on the bridge before. I'd always been stuck in my quarters, or up in the dome. It was an honor to be on the battle bridge with the full warriors, the princes, and the captain himself.

It was because I was Elfangor's little brother. An *aristh* like me, a warrior-cadet, wouldn't have been on the bridge otherwise.

Especially not an *aristh* who had once run into Captain Nerefir so hard he'd fallen over and ended up bruising one of his eye stalks. It was an accident, but still, it's just not a good idea for lowly cadets to go plowing into great heroes.

But everyone loved Elfangor, so they had to tolerate me. That's the story of my life. If I live two hundred years, I'll probably still be known as Elfangor's little brother.

We came out of Z-Space or zero space, a realm of white emptiness, back into normal space. Through the monitors I saw nothing but blackness dotted with stars. And there, just ahead of us, no more than a half-million miles away, was a small, mostly blue planet.

<Is that Earth?> I asked Elfangor. <I didn't realize there was so much water. Can you get Old Hoof and Tail to let me go down to the planet with you?>

<Aximili, shut up!> Elfangor said quickly. He looked slightly sick and cast a dubious glance at Captain Nerefir.

I guess I had been thought-speaking a little loudly. Elfangor was worried that War-Prince Nerefir might have overheard. But I was sure I hadn't been that loud. I mean, I really didn't think that —

<Old Hoof and Tail, eh?> Captain Nerefir said. <Is that what they call me?>

Elfangor shot me a poisonous look. <I'm sure this *aristh* didn't mean any disrespect.>

I think my brother would have liked to throw me out of the nearest airlock right at that moment.

Slowly Nerefir turned his two main eyes toward me. He was a frightening old Andalite. A great warrior. A great hero. Elfangor's idol. <Ah, it's the ruffian. The wild brat who knocked me over.> He nodded. <Old Hoof and Tail, is it? Well. I kind of like the name.> He slowly winked one eye at Elfangor. <I suppose we'll have to let the ruffian live.>

Suddenly . . .

<Yeerks! We have a Yeerk mother ship in orbit over the planet!> the warrior at the sensor station cried.

<They're launching fighters! I count twelve Yeerk Bug fighters,> another warrior cried. <They're on an intercept course. They'll be in firing range in twelve Earth minutes.>

Captain Nerefir turned his face and his main eyes toward my brother, while his stalk eyes kept watch on the monitors. The humor was gone from his face. <Prince Elfangor? It is time. Launch all fighters.>

But Elfangor hadn't waited for orders. He was already halfway out the door. My tail banged into the doorway as I plowed after him.

<Get to the dome, Aximili,> Elfangor said.

<But I want to fight!> I said. <I can fly a fighter as well as —>

<Do not argue with me, Aximili. *Arisths* do not go into battle. You are not a full warrior yet. Go to the dome. You will be safer there.>

<I don't want to be *safe*,> I said. But a warrior, even a warrior-cadet, has to obey orders. Elfangor was my brother. He was also my prince.

I could hear the thought-speak announcements coming from the bridge:

<Yeerk Bug fighters closing fast.>

<We are entering the outer-gravitational field of the planet.>

Elfangor and I came to a pair of drop shafts. Warriors were zooming down, heading for the fighter bays. I would have to go up to reach the dome. The upward drop shaft was empty.

It made me angry. Everyone was fighting but me. When it was all over, Elfangor would be even more of a big hero, and I would still be the little brother. The child.

Elfangor hesitated for just a moment before rushing on. He arched his tail forward. I reached forward with my own tail, arching it up over my back. We touched tail blades.

<You'll have your chance to fight, Aximili,> my brother said. <Very soon your fighter will fly side

by side with mine. But not in *this* battle.>

<Yes, my prince,> I said, sounding very stiff and formal. But as he turned to enter the drop shaft, I couldn't let him go thinking I was mad at him. I said, <Hey, Elfangor? Go burn some slugs.>

<That's the plan, little brother,> he said with a laugh. <That is the plan.>

It was the last I saw of him.

He disappeared down the drop shaft. I went upward to the great dome. The dome was the heart of our ship. It was a vast, round, open plain of grass and trees and running water from our home planet, all covered by a transparent dome.

I was alone there. The only non-warrior on the great ship. The only one without a battle to fight.

I could see the blue planet above me, hanging in a black sky. It had a moon, just a dead ball of dust. But the planet looked alive. I could see white clouds swirling. Its yellow sun's light sparkled off the vast oceans.

This planet was known to be inhabited by a reasonably intelligent species. We had learned a little about them in school.

My main eyes were drawn to the brilliant flares of engine exhaust as our fighters lanced toward the onrushing Yeerks.

I was far from the battle bridge now, beyond the range of their thought-speak. I heard nothing in my head. And my ears heard only the sound of a gentle, artificial breeze ruffling the leaves of the trees. I stood on blue-green grass and watched tiny pinpoints of light as the battle was joined in orbit above the blue planet.

And then . . . I felt it. A tremor that rolled through my mind. A wave of coldness . . . a premonition. Like a waking nightmare.

I turned my stalk eyes away from battle, toward the dead moon of the blue planet. And there I saw it. A black shape against the gray-white light of the moon. A shape like some twisted battle-ax.

<Blade ship . . .> I whispered. <A Visser's Blade ship!>

Our fighters were all away. Our Dome ship had massive weapons, but the Blade ship was fast and maneuverable. Too fast!

The warriors on the battle bridge had no choice. They had to separate the dome in order to be able to fight. I felt a grinding, crunching sensation as the dome was released to drift free of the main line of the ship.

Then . . . silence as the dome floated free.

Slowly, the rest of my ship rotated into sight. Without the dome it looked like a long stick, with the huge bulge of engines on the far end, and the smaller bulge of the battle bridge in the middle.

They were trying to turn to meet the Blade ship.

Too slow.

The Blade ship fired!

<NO!>

Dracon beams, bright as a sun, lanced through space.

The ship fired again. Again. Again.

An explosion of light! A silent explosion like a small sun going nova.

The ship . . . my ship . . . blew up into its separate atoms. One huge flash of light, and a hundred Andalite warriors died.

WHUMMPPPFF!

The shock wave hit the dome. It was translated into sound. The grass beneath my hooves slammed up at me. A terrible rattling, shaking, heaving.

The dome hurtled at shocking speed down and down and down through the atmosphere. Down toward the sparkling sea.

Crrr-UUUUUSSSSHHH!

The dome hit water! Boiling, steaming water rushed over the dome. I was sinking! Sinking beneath the ocean of the blue planet. I was powerless. Terrified.

Alone.

After an eternity, the dome crunched heavily onto the ocean floor. Looking up, I could barely see the surface of the water a hundred feet or more over the top of the dome.

I climbed shakily to my four hooves. I was standing on a vast, open plain that was a piece of my own planet. A blue-green park, hidden deep beneath an alien sea.

And there I waited for weeks. I sent out thought-speak cries to my brother. I knew he would save me . . . if he still lived.

But in the end, it was not Elfangor who found me. It was five creatures from the planet. Five "humans," as they call themselves.

They were the ones who told me of Elfangor's last minutes of life. He had broken Andalite law and custom by giving these humans the power to morph. I was shocked, but tried to hide it.

And they had witnessed Elfangor's death. His cold-blooded murder, by the Yeerk overlord: Visser Three.

Visser Three, who slaughtered my helpless, wounded brother.

Visser Three, the only Yeerk ever to infest and control an Andalite body.

Visser Three, known to all Andalites as the Abomination. The only Andalite-Controller.

He had killed Elfangor, and I had inherited a terrible burden. By Andalite custom, I would be required to avenge my brother's death.

Someday I would have to kill Visser Three.